The Winnie Stories

The Winnie Stories

Gwendolyn Boyes-Sitler

Epic Press

Belleville, Ontario, Canada

The Winnie Stories

Copyright © 2004, Gwendolyn Boyes-Sitler

All pictures in The Winnie Stories are from a series of original oil paintings by the Canadian artist Gwendolyn Boyes-Sitler.

The Winnie Stories are the sole property of the author, Gwendolyn Boyes-Sitler, and are copyright protected under Certificate of Registration No. 1010555, Canadian Intellectual Property Office. No part of this publication, either stories or pictures, may be reproduced, stored in or introduced into a retrieval system, or transmitted, in any form or by any means (electronic, photocopying, recording or otherwise), without the prior written permission of both the copyright owner and the above publisher of this book.

The front cover is a capsule taken from original oil paintings, by the artist Gwendolyn Boyes-Sitler, entitled, "Winnie and the Big Kids" and "Low Falls" –Vankoughnet, Muskoka.

ISBN 1-55306-814-9
Cherish Creek Studio
1003 Cherish Creek Lane, R.R. # 3, Bracebridge, ON   P1L 1X1
Telephone 705-645-5650 / Email: cherish@muskoka.com

Photography
Matthew Sitler Photography,
1029 Cherish Creek Lane,
RR#3, Bracebridge, ON P1L 1X1
705-645-1324

Digital image preparation The Artstract Co.,
240 –1 Muskoka Road, S.,
Gravenhurst, ON   P1P 1H5
705-687-1510 / files@theartstract.com

Printed in Canada by Epic Press

Epic Press is an imprint of *Essence Publishing*. For more information, contact:
20 Hanna Court, Belleville, Ontario, Canada K8P 5J2
Phone: 1-800-238-6376 • Fax: (613) 962-3055
E-mail: publishing@essencegroup.com • Internet: www.essencegroup.com

Contents

Acknowledgements 06

Preface 07

The 'Winnie' Paintings 09

1. The Legacy – A Prologue 13

2. Celebrate the Day 25

3. Places All 33

4. The Angel Choir 41

5. Magnifying Glasses 55

6. A What? 69

7. Unresolved Issues 79

8. When Dreams Come True 91

9. The Homecoming 99

10. A Quiet Repose 105

11. A Golden Glow 115

12. Changing Times – An Epilogue 125

Acknowledgements

The author is greatly indebted to the following for their guidance, encouragement and insight:

Jim Sitler for his constant encouragement, love and dedication to this entire endeavour and for his computer skills without which this book would not be possible.

Matthew Sitler for his humour, i.e. "Winnie-world", encouragement and for his wonderful photographic skills which make the 'Winnie' paintings come alive in the book.

Justin Sitler for his effervescent encouragement and practical insights concerning the business aspects of this venture and for that added push needed to keep on going.

To my brothers and sisters: Faith (Hope), Trevor (Howard), Graydon (Brandon), Neil (Kyle), Malcolm (Nathan), Elizabeth (Mary Beth), and Ian (Evan), for providing a lifetime of wonderful emotional and humorous experiences that enabled this book to be conceived.

To my parents, Claude and Lila Boyes, for their ever constant guidance and abiding love through the years of my childhood.

To my uncles, Cyril and Bill, who provided the extra parental influence.

To Lottie Turner Elliott Boyes, my paternal Grandmother, whose tremendous love and influence on my life was not totally realized until I began to write this book.

To the many people in the Village of Vankoughnet who provided me with wonderful childhood experiences, insights, and character parallels which were foundational to the writing of these stories.

To Brent Tingey, a true friend for all time, who allowed me to embellish his character with humor and whimsy.

Special thanks is expressed to Janice Thorel Bloomfield for her wonderful editorial skills; to Mark Wigston and The Artstract Co., in Gravenhurst for technical and computer skills and to Matthew Sitler Photography for the amazing photographs of the paintings.

Preface

The Winnie Stories are a collection of stories based on childhood experiences of the author. They are not in any way meant to depict the life and experiences of the characters in any historical or factual way. They are, however, fictional and factual and allow the author to relate and embellish some of her life experiences in a whimsical, emotional and humorous manner.

The 'Winnie' Paintings

"The Village" Vankoughnet, Muskoka, circa 1950's
An idyllic perspective of the Village of Vankoughnet as it was in the 1950's depicting the two churches, the one where Winnie attended in her childhood and the one where the Anglicans went, the General Store, the Black River, High and Low Falls and the homes of friendly folk scattered throughout the countryside.

"Celebrate the Day" First of July Picnic held on the property of the Orange Hall, Vankoughnet, Muskoka, circa 1950's
This annual event drew people not only from the Village but from surrounding towns and villages to celebrate Canada's Birthday with games, contests and races.

"Places All" Square Dance at the Orange Hall, Vankoughnet, Muskoka, circa 1950's
Square dances have been in the past and continue to be to this present day a lively form of community entertainment for the whole family in the Village of Vankoughnet.

"The Angel Choir" Christmas Concert at the Orange Hall, Vankoughnet, Muskoka, circa 1950's
The Christmas concert put on by the children and teacher from the Village School SS # 1, Oakley, was held in the Orange Hall as the space in the school was too limited. Plays, choirs, pageants and recitations were very much a part of the program. A visit from Santa and a large table of delicious food rounded out the evening.

"Winnie's School Days" SS # 1 Oakley, Vankoughnet, Muskoka, circa 1950's
The one room school was of elemental importance to the life of the community. Children from Grades one through eight and sometimes even grades nine and ten studied and learned together. The younger ones learned from the older ones and the older children learned valuable lessons by coaching and being an example for the little ones. A multi-talented teacher was required to keep it all running smoothly.

"The Gathering Place" St. David's Presbyterian Church, Vankoughnet, Muskoka, circa 1950's
The church was a place of music and warmth and wisdom and was in itself a welcome gathering place for one and all. The stalwart faith of many members of the community added to the strength and richness of the life therein. St. David's and St. Stephen's continue to be strong witnesses in the community.

"The Fall Fair" Bracebridge, Muskoka, circa 1950's
The Fall Fair was and continues to be an annual event in the town closest to the artist's childhood home. It was a time of gathering for folks far and wide to enjoy the fruits of the harvest, observe one another's animals and feel the thrill of a midway. The schools in the area marched in the parade through the town, arriving at the fairgrounds and marking the beginning of the fair.

"The General Store" Vankoughnet, Muskoka, circa 1950's

Of primary importance to the small community was the General Store. One could buy anything there from your winter mitts, fabrics for clothing, groceries, gas and even pick up your mail. The store owners were available long hours of the day and night and were never known to turn a needy customer away due to the lateness of the hour. It was a colourful, magical place through the eyes of a young child.

"The Parlour" Bracebridge, Muskoka, circa 1950's

An idyllic perspective of the apartment sitting room at the home of Winnie's great aunt Emma Elliott and grandmother Lottie Boyes. Fond memories of visiting this lovely Victorian setting are indelibly imprinted upon the artist's mind. The apartment was located in a three storey building owned by the Stone family on James Street. It is the present day location of James Street Place.

"Winnie and the Big Kids" Vankoughnet, Muskoka, circa 1950's

The artist grew up in a large family in the 1950's with a total of eight children, five boys and three girls. Winnie was third from the bottom. The five older children were born one right after the other and became known as 'the big kids'. A gap in time separated them from the three younger ones of which Winnie was the oldest. They were referred to as 'the little kids.'

"A Golden Glow" Vankoughnet, Muskoka, circa 1950's

An idyllic re-creation of the artist's home as she remembers it from childhood. The maple syrup bush, the lumber piles, the barn and the log truck were a familiar part of the setting.

"The Lumber Mill" Vankoughnet, Muskoka, circa 1950's

The lumber industry played a big part in the childhood life of the artist. Her father owned a saw mill which ran all summer long and in the winter, logs were cut and drawn from the bush for the next years sawing. There were several lumber mills in operation during the 1950's but the two that stand out in the artist's mind are that of the Boyes family and the Thompson family.

"The Village"
Vankoughnet, Muskoka, circa 1950's

"THE LEGACY - A PROLOGUE"

Winnie was a little girl. Some days she yearned to be a grown-up and some days she wanted to stay just the way she was, forever. Aunt Ann, Grandma's sister, said to Winnie one day, "Winnie, you're growing toward adolescence." Winnie had no idea what adolescence was and furthermore she had no intention whatsoever of going there. Her ultimate goal in life was to grow up eventually.

Winnie was tall for her age and skinny. Her Uncle Will said she had to stand up twice to make a shadow. Winnie lived in the village of Mistymeadow, about thirty miles from Silver Bridge, past the village of Gruffington, in the township of Oak Leaf. The Misty River ran through her village. It had two falls and two bridges. There was Mr. Hall's General Store and a one-room schoolhouse; two churches, Winnie's church and the one where the Anglicans went; and of course the Orange Hall. Her father's lumber mill was on the edge of the village and also on the edge of the river. There were houses dotted here and there across the landscape and Winnie knew everyone who lived in them. Mrs. Mingey, who lived across the road from Winnie, had an ice cream parlour in the front of her house.

Winnie was the third youngest of a big family with five brothers and two sisters. Her sister Hope was the oldest in the family, "the first born" Grandma would say, and then came Howard, Brandon, Kyle and Nathan. Four boys, one right after the other, like steps on a stepladder. Then there was a little reprieve and along came Winnie, then Mary Beth, and the youngest was Evan. Winnie felt like her family was divided in two because everyone called the older ones from Nathan up "the big kids," while Winnie, Mary Beth and Evan were constantly reminded that they were the "little kids." Being part of either group had both its advantages and disadvantages, Winnie figured. Sometimes the big kids got to go places and to do things that the little ones weren't allowed, but on the other hand much more was expected of them when it came time for doing chores.

Winnie's dad was tall and strong and owned a lumber mill. In the wintertime he was also a logger and he built cottages in the off-season. Winnie's mother had come to Mistymeadow as a young schoolteacher. She had lived in the city but when the opportunity presented itself she jumped at the chance to teach at a rural school. She had been young and pretty and had had sparkling brown eyes. When Winnie's dad saw her for the first time he made up his mind then and there that he was going to marry her, that's if she agreed, of course.

Well, needless to say, they were of the same accord and after a brief time of courting they were married in the minister's house in Silver Bridge on a cold December day. Winnie thought this must have been very romantic, as she pictured her mother and father in a horse-drawn sleigh going off to exchange their wedding vows.

Life had changed dramatically for Winnie's mother. She came back with her new husband to live in the family home along with his parents, his two brothers, Winnie's Uncle Cecil and Uncle Will, and with other relatives constantly coming and going.

As the family grew, the little farmhouse seemed to become smaller and smaller. One day Winnie's dad announced he was going to build a new house a little farther into the village. It would be a house big enough for all of them at the time and could accommodate any more who came along.

Winnie was born on a frosty February morning in the hospital in Silver Bridge. Mamma had to go into Silver Bridge a few days early and stay with Aunt Ann in case Winnie put in an early appearance. However, Winnie arrived on time. She came into the world kicking and screaming with white-blonde hair and eyes so dark and sparkling Uncle Will thought she looked like she'd come from another continent. Winnie wiggled from the time she was born and this was something that set her apart from the other kids: she could not stay still.

Winnie was just a little baby when Daddy was finishing the new house. Even before its completion they all moved in. Winnie shared a room with Hope. Uncle Will and Uncle Cecil shared a room, as did Grandma and Grandpa and, of course, Winnie's mother and dad. The boys all shared a big room on the third floor of this wonderful new house. And sometimes when Winnie's dad hired extra men to help with the logging, they too shared a room in the attic.

It was a busy household and before Winnie could even remember, her grandpa died. "Gone to heaven," Winnie's dad explained. He was "laid to rest" her older brother Brandon told her, in the little cemetery at Winnie's church. Then along came Mary Beth and eventually Evan. When Mary Beth got a little older, she and Winnie shared a room, and Hope, who was practically a grown-up, got to have her own room.

Uncle Cecil and Uncle Will were always part of Winnie's family. They didn't get married and have children of their own. "Lost loves," Winnie's dad said. Winnie and her brothers and sisters were expected to obey their uncles just as they were their mother and father. Uncle Cecil loved children and spent many hours carrying the little ones around trying to pacify them if they were upset about something. Uncle Will was kind too, but a little gruff. He expected that when he asked Winnie to do something she would immediately obey. This didn't always happen, much to Uncle Will's chagrin.

Apart from her mother and father, Grandma was Winnie's favourite adult. Winnie could tell Grandma anything and she would listen and give Winnie a good answer. Grandma was kind to Winnie and even when Winnie was blue she had a special way of cheering her up. Grandma had come from the "homeland" she would tell Winnie, and she was always very proud of her heritage. Grandma had a twin sister, Aunt Ann, who was a nurse. Winnie liked Aunt Ann but thought she was a little too strict.

Beyond this immediate family there was a multitude of aunts and uncles and cousins on both Mamma's and Daddy's sides of the family. No matter what the holiday there would be lots of relatives visiting at Winnie's house.

Sometimes Winnie felt overwhelmed at having so many people in her home all the time. She found a little rock on a hill not too far away and, when life got too hectic for Winnie to deal with, she would go and sit on her rock and ponder her circumstances. From there Winnie could view most of the village of Mistymeadow. She could see Mr. Hall coming and going from his general store. She could watch her brothers and sisters working and playing at her own house. Sometimes she would see Mr. Mingey, her neighbour, and his sons Trent and Marlin burning the long grass in the field beside their house.

One time she watched in horror as the fire got out of control and the flames started lapping right up around the Mingey's house. She saw Mrs. Mingey run outside calling to Winnie's dad and uncles and the older boys to come and help put it out. Winnie saw Hope with a pan of water in each hand running across the road to help. But before she could make it there, the water had all spilled out. However, with the help of Winnie's family and a few other neighbours the fire was soon extinguished and the Mingey's house was saved. That night Winnie's dad gave them all a very serious talk around the supper table as to the hazards of being careless with fire. Winnie knew there was more to her dad's warning than just the Mingey's fire. One time he himself had thrown an old wicker chair into the fireplace at their new house. It had burned so quickly and with such a ferocious roar that even Winnie's dad, who was never fearful of anything, appeared a little pale.

Sometimes from her rock, if Winnie squinted really hard, she could see her friends Beryl and Mandy playing in the field at their grandmother's house across the river. Every summer these friends came from the city to visit in Winnie's village. Winnie loved to play with them and mostly she loved to swim with them in the river. Beryl and Mandy were cousins to each other and their mothers were sisters. They spent most of their time sitting on the beach. Winnie and Mary Beth loved to finish their chores quickly and go and spend the afternoon with them. Mandy's mother taught them how to swim. When the fall weather came, Beryl and Mandy and their families would return to the city and Winnie wouldn't see them until the next summer.

Winnie's family always had animals. There were the barn animals, of course. The horses, Prince and Trigger, were used at the mill to help skid the logs and then in the winter they would pull the big, heavy logs out of the bush. The only real connection Winnie had with the horses was in the late summer, when the millwork was done, Prince and Trigger would be pastured in the fenced-in field beside Winnie's house. Trigger had a wart on the end of his nose and he was always trying to open the gate with it and get into the yard.

"Make sure that gate is closed properly," Winnie's dad would constantly remind everyone in the family. But inevitably Trigger would get into the yard at the house and eat a lot of Mamma's marigolds.

Winnie remembered a very sad time with the team of horses before Prince and Trigger when Uncle Will had been crossing the lake on the frozen ice with the horses and a big load of logs. Suddenly a crack appeared in the ice and the weight of the horses was too much. Uncle Will tried his best to get them across the crack but it was all in vain and the horses were lost. That was the closest Winnie had ever come to seeing Uncle Will cry.

Winnie's dad had put his arm around him and said, "You did your best, Will, and no one could have done more. Life deals these blows sometimes and we may never understand why." Grandma had made a big pot of tea and Winnie and her brothers and sisters gave Uncle Will lots of hugs over the next few days.

Winnie's family had cows too. There was the Jersey cow and the Guernsey cow and a little cow called Daisy. Winnie didn't know what kind she was but she liked her best. Every evening Winnie's brothers took turns milking the cows. Sometimes they let Winnie help but she wasn't particularly adept at this.

"You have no patience, Winnie," Brandon would say. "The cow has to be relaxed and calm to give milk. When you try, Winnie, it's as if the cow is being milked by a butterfly. You flit around and about and don't have enough strength to do the job."

Winnie was a little offended but, since milking a cow wasn't high on her priority list, she really wasn't going to let Brandon's comments affect her for very long. The thing she liked most about the cows was the little bell each one wore around her neck. Winnie had thought the bells were just so the cows would sound nice but her brother Kyle soon set her straight.

"Really, Winnie, do you think the cows are going to form a bell choir?" he chided. "The bells are so if any of them gets lost we know where to look for them. We just listen for the sound of the bell and follow it." Winnie liked the idea of a bell choir better.

The animal that received the most attention from Winnie's family was the dog, Ranger. He was a Border Collie and, although he was helpful in rounding up the cows from time to time, mostly he was the family pet. Ranger had to share his time with eight children and so, of course, by the end of the day he was content to lie on the hearth and not pay attention to anyone. Ranger's reputation was far-reaching. He was the only dog in all of Oak Leaf Township that could run ten feet straight up a tree when someone threw a snowball at the tree. Often in winter, when people were visiting at Winnie's house, they would ask her brothers to get Ranger to do this. Winnie loved Ranger because he was always gentle and always willing to play a game of chasing the ball or willing to let Winnie use him as a pillow. Whatever Winnie's needs were at the moment, Ranger was usually there to try to meet them, especially when everyone else seemed to have something more important to do, or so they thought.

One day when Ranger was getting old he just disappeared. Winnie woke up one morning and Ranger was gone.

"Where is he?" Winnie asked with desperation in her voice. Everyone seemed too calm about it. "Why weren't they outside looking for him?" Winnie wondered.

"Ranger just melted in the sun," Uncle Cecil said in his kindest voice.

Even Winnie, who was accused of believing almost anything, knew this was impossible. "Dogs don't melt. They're not snowmen," Winnie stated emphatically.

Grandma, who always told Winnie the way things really were, put her arm around Winnie's shoulder and guided her aside from the others.

"Winnie," Grandma said, "Ranger was an old dog. He lived a lot of really good years. He was a big help to all of us but mostly he was a dear friend. But, Winnie," she continued, "Ranger didn't have any strength left and he just slept peacefully away."

Winnie knew that Grandma meant that Ranger had died and she knew that Grandma hated to have to tell her. Winnie was very sad but at least she knew where Ranger was and the fact that he had died was easier for her to accept than if Ranger had melted.

Life was just a continuation of events for Winnie. There were so many things going on all of the time. Some were happy things and some were sad, and some were just things. There was a sad time in Winnie's life when she was ten years old. She and Trent Mingey were riding their tricycles on the front veranda.

"Keep your tricycle on the ground, Winnie, and don't be riding it up on the veranda," Winnie's dad had warned her.

Winnie tried hard to be obedient but sometimes the temptation to follow others was too great for her. When Trent Mingey said he had no problem with riding his tricycle on the porch, Winnie felt she couldn't let him think she didn't have the nerve. The veranda was open space with no railings on it and, sure enough, Winnie rode her tricycle right off the side. Her injury was severe and she ended up spending several weeks in the hospital in Silver Bridge yes, the very same one she'd been born in.

Not even once did Winnie's dad say, "Winnie, I warned you about that." But Winnie knew she'd learned a lesson. She just wished she hadn't had to learn it the hard way.

Winnie's favourite pastime was reading. She loved it when the lending library would come to her school and bring a whole rash of new books for Winnie to choose from. She was always on her best behaviour that day so that the teacher would let her get to the library box quickly and have first choice of what was available. She liked it best when the books arrived on a Friday and she could take home several with the whole weekend ahead of her to read. Winnie also spent a lot of her time writing stories and drawing pictures. Mamma constantly had to tell her to get her chores done before losing herself in some frivolous activity.

"Winnie," Grandma would say, "someday, you're going to be a great painter or poet or maybe a writer of wonderful stories."

Winnie would smile. She hoped that Grandma was right but mostly in her heart she thought she'd have to do something practical before she could get to these other things. "Live from your heart and these other things will take care of themselves." Grandma's words made Winnie feel encouraged.

"Live from your heart," Winnie repeated inside her head. That's what she intended to do.

Mrs. Mingey's Carrot Pudding

1 cup grated raw carrots
1 cup grated raw potato
1 1/2 cups bread flour
1 cup brown sugar
1 cup suet [or butter]
1 cup seedless raisins
1 cup currants
1/2 teaspoon cloves
1/2 teaspoon nutmeg
1/2 teaspoon cinnamon

1 teaspoon baking soda

Grate carrot and potato. Measure and set aside.
Crumble suet, add the sugar and blend well. Add to this the carrot and only half of the potato and mix well.

Sprinkle fruits with flour and add to first mixture. Then add the flour and spices which have been sifted together. Dissolve soda in the remaining last half cup of potato and add it at the last. Mix lightly together. Pour into buttered bowls. Tie down and steam or boil for three hours.

"Celebrate the Day"
First of July Picnic held on the property of the Orange Hall, Vankoughnet, Muskoka, circa 1950's

"CELEBRATE THE DAY"

Winnie awoke with a jolt. A great thunderclap crashed outside her bedroom window. Beads of rain pelted down the glass panes and streaks of lightning flashed through the sky. Winnie was devastated. Today was the First of July. Every year her entire family, along with all the other families in the village of Mistymeadow and beyond, even as far away as Gruffington, gathered for a big picnic on the lawn at the Orange Hall.

Winnie thought about how Mr. and Mrs. Mingey set up a refreshment stand where they sold ice cream cones and pop of all different kinds. Winnie's favourite pop was red cream soda. One time she had drunk the whole bottle so fast she burped for ten minutes straight. She thought that would impress her older brothers. Her big sister, Hope, was horrified. "Winnie," she said, "if going anywhere with me is important to you, you need to learn some manners."

Winnie loved Hope and wouldn't want to do anything to upset her, so right there and then that very day she had resolved within herself to learn the meaning of the word "etiquette." Hope said anyone going places in the world needed to know proper etiquette. And Winnie always felt she was definitely headed somewhere.

Winnie remembered how some of the men got involved in log sawing contests. The cross-cut saw contest was a favourite, with two men, one on either end of the saw, working till the sweat ran down their faces in an attempt to cut through a big log in record time. Kyle and Nathan, two of Winnie's older brothers, liked to compete with some of the Perry boys but her brothers were no match for them. They had a big steer at their place to contend with while Winnie's brothers only had the Jersey cow. Looking after farm animals built up great strength. And definitely strength was what was needed to win the cross-cut saw contest.

Winnie's favourite event was running races. "Winnie runs like the wind," she had heard Uncle Cecil say once and so Winnie prided herself on being able to win the race.

She and Trent, the youngest of the Mingey boys, who was the same age as Winnie, competed with each other constantly. He told Winnie he was better than she at everything but when it came to running she knew she could win.

"How do you run so fast?" Trent asked her one day when they were walking home from school.

"It's because I was born with angel wings," Winnie answered. Trent let out a big guffaw and walked on ahead of Winnie. Winnie smiled smugly.

Three-legged races where you tied one of your legs to the leg of another person your size, and moved in a combination of running and hopping toward the finish line, brought much laughter from onlookers. Mary Beth and Evan, Winnie's little sister and brother, along with other little children loved to get into old potato sacks and hop as best they could to finish the race. Many falls and having to re-establish themselves in the sacks were all part of the fun. Evan took many tumbles and Winnie watched as Mary Beth with her kind little heart stopped to pick him up.

The biggest event of the day was always the tug-of-war. Winnie's dad, her uncles and brothers, and any other men who worked at her dad's lumber mill were in competition with all the men who worked at the other local saw mill. Each team lined up on either end of the big hemp rope, grasping firmly with their strong, tanned arms and their feet braced firmly in the ground. The Perry family was so big they had men on both teams. Winnie would watch as each team pulled and pulled.

"Now, stand back, Winnie," her father would say, "or you'll get knocked to the ground if the men lose their grip." Winnie would stand back and then gradually edge her way forward again. One time Mr. Mosley actually stepped right on her left foot.

The muscles on the men's arms would bulge and their faces got redder and redder. Often the men who weighed the most were positioned on each end of the rope. Uncle Will on one end and Norman Mosley on the other provided the anchor for each team. Finally after much grunting and groaning, one team would pull the other across the dividing line. The teams were so evenly matched there was never any assurance in advance as to which one would win. However, once the winner was announced the men would all congratulate each other with a handshake and great guffaws and laughter. Winnie loved to watch the camaraderie.

Winnie swung her feet onto the floor as another loud clap of thunder rattled the windows. Just then Ranger, the family dog, took a huge leap onto Winnie's bed and buried his nose in the covers. Mary Beth sat bolt upright. "What's going on, Winnie?" she queried.

Winnie didn't even take the time to answer; she just motioned to Mary Beth to get out of bed. Winnie could hear voices in the kitchen. She scrambled to get into her clothes and raced downstairs to see what the commotion was all about.

Mr. Hall and Mr. Mingey along with several other neighbours had gathered in the kitchen with Winnie's dad and Uncle Will and Uncle Cecil. Mamma and Hope were busy frying bacon and eggs. The older boys, Howard, Brandon, Kyle and Nathan, were in and out doing chores and listening in on as much of the conversation as possible.

"Well, we have lots of tarps at the mill," Winnie's dad was saying. "We can attach those to the trees."

"And we could open up the Orange Hall and anyone wanting to stay dry could go inside there," Mr. Hall chimed in.

"And we're fine for refreshments," added Mr. Mingey. "The stand pretty well covers everything and maybe we could build a little fire outside where we can heat up some hot drinks for the older folks," he continued.

Winnie felt a tiny ray of hope filter through her.

"Would they even consider holding the picnic if the storm continued?" Winnie wanted to break into the conversation with her question, but from past experience she decided that it was better to keep quiet when adults were trying to make up their minds. Besides she was trying to practise her "etiquette."

Just then Grandma came into the kitchen. She was putting on a freshly pressed apron over her housedress. In her quiet manner she went about pouring coffee and listening to the ongoing conversation. When she decided to interject, everyone stopped to listen.

"There are some things that need to be celebrated," Grandma said, "and being part of this wonderful country is one of them." Grandma had left her native land as a young girl and had come with her family to live here in this country. She had met Grandpa, a young lumberjack, and they had been married in the little country church on Christmas Day many years before.

"We need to raise the flag, lift our voices and celebrate the day. A little stormy weather didn't stop our ancestors and we mustn't let it stop us," Grandma continued.
"Well, then the decision is made," Winnie's dad declared. "The First of July picnic is on!"

Great cheers went up from Winnie and her brothers and sisters. It was as if life went on to fast-forward as the chores were completed, the tarps erected, and the refreshment stand prepared.

Winnie watched as one by one people began to arrive. Colourful umbrellas could be seen dotting the landscape. Children in their shiny slickers and rubber boots splashed in the puddles. Mr. Moriarty came in his wheelchair and brought his guitar. He would be playing for the square dance later that evening and wouldn't need to go home in between. The excitement and the anticipation of the people far outweighed the dampness of the weather. As more and more people filtered in, Winnie watched as Mr. Hall raised the flag and then Mrs. Burbridge's voice was heard as others joined in with,

O Canada!
Our home and native land!
True patriot love in all thy sons command.
With glowing hearts we see thee rise,
The True North strong and free!
From far and wide,
O Canada, we stand on guard for thee.

Winnie felt so proud she thought that her heart was going to burst. She stood straight and tall and raised her eyes to the flag. Some of the men placed their hands over their hearts as the flag was raised. "They are home from the war," Mamma quietly squelched Winnie's inquisitive look.

Suddenly a little ray of sunlight broke out from behind a cloud and beamed across the Union Jack. "It will be a fine First of July picnic," Winnie thought. She looked at Grandma just as a tear trickled down her cheek but not once did Grandma's eyes stray from the flag. Mrs. Burbridge's voice continued,

God keep our land glorious and free!
O Canada, we stand on guard for thee.
O Canada, we stand on guard for thee.

Great shouts of "Hurrah!" went up from voices everywhere. "Let the picnic begin," chortled Mr. Mingey in a voice that was barely audible over the sounds of the noisy crowd.

Winnie shivered with excitement as she watched the picnic begin to unfold. The races were run; the contests were held. Winnie, as usual, beat Trent Mingey in the running race. Mary Beth and Evan each fell four times during the sack race and in the end lost out to little Mona Toll. The Perry boys came first in the cross-cut saw contest and Winnie's dad's lumber mill succumbed to the opposing team in the tug of war. "We're no match for Norman Mosley," Winnie's dad said with a sly grin.

At the end of the day the tarps were folded and put away, the refreshment stand was closed and the lawn was cleared up.

Winnie's dad proclaimed, "It was the best First of July ever!" Winnie agreed.

"Places All"
Square Dance at the Orange Hall, Vankoughnet, Muskoka, circa 1950's

"PLACES ALL"

Winnie tiptoed about the house in an uncommon manner. She desperately wanted to go to the square dance at the Orange Hall, but she had asked so many times that her father had said, "Winnie, if you ask me again the answer will be no!" She thought if she was on her best behaviour and became almost invisible it would please him and she would be allowed to go.

She could hear the music in her head: the fiddle, the banjo, the guitar and Mrs. Burbridge on the piano. She could hear the caller "Places all, all over the hall." Sometimes her big brother Brandon would call, but he was just learning so it was only when the regular callers needed a break that they called on him.

Winnie loved going to the square dance and, after all, it was just across the road from her house. Her big sister, Hope, and her older brothers were allowed to go but Winnie was at that in-between age where she could only attend if her father went also.

Sometimes some of the men got a little out of control and would get into a fistfight outside the Hall. Mamma said it was because they'd been in the bush too long and had forgotten how to act like gentlemen. But mostly the square dances were filled with lively music and laughter. Sometimes Mrs. Burbridge and her daughter Willa would sing between sets. Winnie loved it when they sang "The Martins and the Coys, they were reckless mountain boys." Everyone would be tapping their toes and clapping to their voices. Sometimes Willa would break into the song "Beautiful, beautiful brown eyes, beautiful, beautiful brown eyes." Winnie had even heard Willa sing that on the radio. She pretended that she was singing about her because Winnie, like all of her brothers and sisters, had brown eyes of course.

Winnie wondered at what age she would be allowed to go on her own and be one of the big kids. She always had to wait for Daddy to make his decision and then usually Mary Beth and Evan, Winnie's little sister and brother, got to go too.

"Winnie," her father called from the kitchen. "Winnie, are you not feeling well? You're so quiet!"

"Oh, no," Winnie thought as she ran to her father. "Had her plan backfired?"

Winnie was always such a chatterbox. Mr. Meeks, the handy man, had even nicknamed her that because he thought she never stopped talking.

"I'm feeling fine," Winnie was quick to respond.

"Well, then," said her father, "round up Mary Beth and Evan and when everyone is ready we'll go to the square dance." Winnie was gleeful. She hugged her father and ran to tell the other kids.

"What will I wear?" she questioned her mother. "Can I wear the pink dress that Grandma made?" she pleaded.

"Oh, Winnie, that dress is for going to church," her mother responded.

"Please, just this once?" Winnie persisted.

"Well, be very careful with it," her mother conceded with a smile.

Allemande left to the corners all,

Right to your honey and grand chain all.

Dip and dive to the ocean wave,

Inside over and outside under,

You go over and I'll go under,

Roll 'em around like a crack of thunder….

The Orange Hall was alive with colour and people and movement and music. Winnie's eyes were huge as she took in the full impact of the evening. It was just as Winnie had envisioned. The dancers were tapping their toes to the music and moving one from the other, back and forth, swinging around till some of the women were swept off their feet. Squeals of delight and jovial laughter reached Winnie's ears. Mr. Mingey and his pretty wife, who spoke with an accent, were there along with Mr. and Mrs. Hall. Winnie had never seen Mr. Hall move so fast in all her life. Mr. Hall ran the General Store and his wife was the school teacher. Winnie knew Mr. Hall liked music.

Sometimes, when Mamma would let Winnie, Mary Beth and Evan go down the road to the store to buy red liquorice, Mr. Hall would say, "How about a song today, Evan?" It didn't matter what time of year it was, Evan would sing his favourite song "Rudolph the Red-Nosed Reindeer." Mr. Hall would chuckle to himself and give each of them a lollypop. Winnie and Mary Beth thought they were very lucky that little Evan could sing so well.

Mr. Moriarty, who lived on the corner where the four roads diverged, was sitting in his wheelchair waiting to be carried up on the stage. "He suffered a dreadful disease as a young man," Grandma had told Winnie when she had asked why he couldn't walk. But Winnie knew he could play the guitar beautifully.

Howard and Kyle and Nathan, Winnie's older brothers, were taking a turn at playing the instruments. Winnie had heard Uncle Will say that Kyle had a real feel for the fiddle. Uncle Will had taught him to play "Turkey in the Straw" and sometimes on Saturday night they would stand around the piano in the living room and play the fiddle while Mamma chorded on the piano and the other boys took turns at the guitar and banjo.

The lights were so bright in the Orange Hall that the moths flew around and around them in time to the music it seemed to Winnie. One time Winnie had seen a young fellow from the city actually breathe in a moth when he was dancing. The poor fellow choked and sputtered and couldn't get his breath. Some of the older men had taken him outside for some fresh air, Winnie supposed.

Some of the girls who were working at the local tourist lodge had walked to the dance. Winnie could see them smiling and giggling at her older brothers, hoping to be asked to dance and to get a ride home, Winnie guessed. There was no shortage of young men asking Hope to dance either. But Hope didn't appear to take any of them seriously.

"There's only one right person for each of us," Grandma always said. Hope would make certain she kept all her options open so she would be available when "Mr. Right" did come along. Winnie thought Hope had her eye on Christos, the dark haired young man who preached at the little church on Sundays. But he didn't come to the square dances, of course.

There would be lots of things for Winnie and Mary Beth to talk about when they fell into bed tonight.

Winnie stayed pretty close to her father, not wanting to get trampled by the dancers. Suddenly a new set was beginning. The caller shouted out "Places all!" Dancers gathered on the floor, coming from every direction. Winnie noticed him coming toward her.

"Oh, no," she thought, "I hope he's coming to speak to Daddy."

But he was looking right at Winnie. Mr. Mingey, not the one married to the lady with the accent, but the one who lived across the road from Winnie, came and asked her to dance. Winnie wanted to disappear. She couldn't make herself get out on the dance floor and actually move with the other dancers.

"Go ahead, Winnie. Give it a try," her father encouraged.

Winnie felt even her father had forsaken her at that moment. Before she knew it, Winnie was being pushed and guided and twirled and pulled here and there and around and back. The caller was saying,

Take that lady by the wrist
And take her for a grapevine twist.

Winnie was dizzy; her face felt as red and hot as Uncle Will's looked when the doctor had told him he had high blood pressure.

Winnie felt out of control. She was totally at the mercy of the other dancers in a long chain moving and twisting about the dance floor. Suddenly she was back beside Mr. Mingey and he was swinging her around and around till her feet would no longer stay on the floor. Winnie tried to catch her breath but the caller continued:

Place those ladies back to back
And gents go round the outside track.
Elbow swing with the one you swung
And swing the next on the run.

"Would this ever end?" Winnie felt panicky as once again she was twirled round and round the dance floor. After what seemed like forever the music stopped and Mr. Mingey smiled at Winnie as she scampered back to her father.

Mary Beth and Evan were beside themselves with giggles as they embraced Winnie. "Oh, Winnie, you were dancing!" Mary Beth exclaimed with a look of admiration and awe in her eyes. Evan danced around Winnie wanting her to take him out on the dance floor.

Winnie blinked back the tears of embarrassment she had been feeling. Suddenly she realized that in the eyes of Mary Beth and Evan, she had just made the giant leap to becoming one of the big kids.

Winnie looked up at her father. He was smiling down at her and with a big wink said, "Well done, Winnie!"

"The Angel Choir"
Christmas Concert at the Orange Hall, Vankoughnet, Muskoka, circa 1950's

"THE ANGEL CHOIR"

Winnie fought back the tears. She would not let anyone see her cry. Night after night she had lain in bed hoping upon hope that Mrs. Hall would choose her for the angel choir in the Christmas concert.

Mamma always said, "You can do anything in life you choose to do, Winnie."

She had envisioned herself standing on the stage in her white, filmy costume with wings as transparent as those of butterflies and a beautiful tinsel halo on her silky, blonde hair. She would sing with the others in their heavenly voices and the audience would be awed into silence. She could see it all now, "a dozen angels" Mrs. Hall had said. Surely there would be room for Winnie.

Hark! the herald angels sing,
"Glory to the new born King!…"

Winnie knew the words already. She had been practising as she dawdled behind the others on her way home from school. She wanted to surprise her older brothers at how well she could sing.

Today Mrs. Hall had called out the names of the girls for the angel choir. Winnie had held her breath: Marjie, Jeanette, Tina Mae, Audrey and on and on it went, right down to Mary Beth. Yes, Mary Beth, her little sister who had only begun school this past September would be in the angel choir.

"There must be some mistake," Winnie thought as she counted out the names over and over. Mrs. Hall had only named eleven and there were to be twelve angels.

"Mrs. Hall," Winnie raised her hand.

"Yes, Winnie," she responded.

"You forgot one."

"Oh," Mrs. Hall replied, "I am asking Hope to come and help us out for the concert. We can use her lovely alto voice."

Hope was Winnie's older sister and she was nearly finished high school. Winnie loved Hope and was pleased to think she'd be part of the concert. She knew Mrs. Hall had also asked Howard, Winnie's oldest brother, to return from high school and play the part of Scrooge in the "Cratchett's Family Christmas" play.

There had been no mistake. Winnie felt the tears stinging her eyes.

The next few weeks were filled with activity. There were garlands to be made, bows to be tied, and costumes to be put together. Mamma was going through the closets, collecting housecoats, scarves and bandannas. Mary Beth's little doll was to be the baby Jesus. Kyle, Winnie's brother, and a girl named Mary, from the grade six class, were to be Joseph and Mary. Winnie thought it very appropriate that Mary already had the proper name. Winnie and an older girl, Tina Mae, were asked to make the tinsel halos for the choir. One by one they cut the tinsel and taped the ends together making them different sizes so there would be a halo to fit the large and the small.

Winnie didn't feel that her heart was in it. She was doing her best to help with everything she could.

"Winnie, disappointments are part of life," Mamma said when Winnie tried to tell her how much she wanted to be an angel.

Hope knew that Winnie was disappointed and had gone to Mrs. Hall to ask her to let Winnie have her place, but Mrs. Hall had said she was sorry about it but the younger girls really needed Hope's voice to help them along.

The evenings were quiet at home. Hope and the older boys had homework to do and lots of exams before the Christmas holidays. Mary Beth and Evan, Winnie's little brother, had to go to bed earlier than Winnie. At least that was one thing in her favour, Winnie thought. Winnie's dad was very quiet too. He hadn't said anything to Winnie about the angel choir but she was sure he knew. He knew things that Winnie thought were impossible for him to know. He was spending a lot of time in the evenings writing at Uncle Cecil's desk. It must be something to do with the tally sheets, Winnie guessed.

She knew tally sheets were very important to someone in the lumber business. One time when she was very small she had taken a tally sheet off of Uncle Cecil's desk thinking it would be fun to play with. There had been so much commotion and upset with everyone in the family being called upon to look for it that Winnie had hidden it under the porch at the back of the house. Her brother Brandon had found it and there was great rejoicing that the tally sheet was recovered and returned to its rightful spot on Uncle Cecil's desk.

"It's that darn dog!" Uncle Cecil had exclaimed. "He must have taken it off my desk and hidden it outside."

Winnie had remained very quiet. She hated to have Ranger blamed for such an awful deed but since it appeared that he wasn't going to be scolded any further she felt it best to leave things as they were. It wasn't until later Winnie revealed the truth to Kyle and, of course, he could hardly wait to tell the story, but by then no one was very upset.

Mamma was busy sewing at her machine. Aunt Eileen, Mamma's sister, had given her a red velvet dress that had belonged to her daughter Maggie. Winnie assumed that Mamma was making something for Mary Beth.

It was only eight days before the Christmas concert. The preparations were almost completed. Winnie had helped gather pine boughs and would help Mr. Hall and her brothers put them up in the Orange Hall for decoration. The Orange Hall was across the road from Winnie's house and when special events happened in Winnie's village this was usually where they took place. It was bigger than Winnie's school and had a stage and real chairs for people to sit on. All kinds of important things went on in the Orange Hall. When Winnie's father became the reeve, people went there to vote for him. Several times during the summer, square dances were held and Winnie loved to be able to go. But her most favourite of all was the First of July picnic with races and tug-of-war and an ice cream booth. Winnie and her brothers and sisters were allowed to have orange pop and red cream soda on that particular day.

Winnie's father got up from the desk where he was doing the tally sheets, or so Winnie thought. "Winnie," he called out, "I have something to ask you about." Winnie, pleased to have some attention, ran over to him.

"I saw Mrs. Hall in the grocery store today. She said if there was a special Christmas poem or recitation that you could memorize before the concert, she would be pleased to have you recite it at the closing of the programme."

Winnie was stunned. "Me?" she asked.

"Yes, you, Winnie."

"But what would I ever recite and how can I learn it between now and the concert?" she queried.

"I have written a little poem for you, Winnie, and I think that if you and I practise it every night between now and then you will do just fine."

Winnie's mind was swirling. She, Winnie, reciting a poem, all on her own at the end of the concert was just so exciting to think about. Already she felt that funny shaking inside her that she always got when she had to do something important on her own.

"But Daddy," she questioned, "what poem will I give?"

Then her dad retrieved some bits of paper from Uncle Cecil's desk. "I've put a few lines together here, Winnie, and when I work on it a little more it should be ready just for you."

Winnie read the poem over and over. It was wonderful. "The Ringing of the Bells," it was called. It brought tears to Winnie's eyes it was so beautiful. But they weren't like those other tears, ones of disappointment. These were tears of love for her dad and tears of emotion for the words he had written.

Each night after supper Winnie and her father practised the poem. "Stand tall, Winnie, and speak out loud and clear," her father instructed.

Winnie memorized the words in no time and with each practice session she felt more and more comfortable.

The afternoon of the concert arrived. Winnie and her brothers and sisters went off for the dress rehearsal. Nathan was a king, Kyle was Joseph, Brandon was Mr. Cratchett, and Howard, of course, was Scrooge. Hope took Mary Beth's hand along with their angel costumes and crossed the road to the Orange Hall. Winnie followed along. She didn't really need a costume for her poem.

The rehearsal went well. A few of the older folks from the village came to watch, as going out at night was too tiring for them. Winnie recited the poem without any mistakes and Mrs. Hall said she sounded very good.

Finally the evening arrived. Winnie was putting on her pink dress that Grandma had made for her to wear to church. Mamma appeared at the door of her room. "What about this one, Winnie?"

There before her very eyes was the most beautiful red velvet dress Winnie had ever seen. It was silky-soft when she touched it and it had a beautiful lacy white collar and cuffs and trim to match at the bottom. Winnie was breathless.

"Oh, Mamma!" she exclaimed. "I thought that you were making something for Mary Beth."

"There was enough material to make a little one for her too, Winnie, but this one is for you."

Winnie felt those tears again as she hugged Mamma and said, "Thank you!"

Just then Grandma appeared at the door. "I think you need these too, Winnie," she said as she handed Winnie her beautiful creamy white pearls. "You'll need to wrap them around twice but they should look lovely on your red dress."

Winnie was ecstatic! She quickly put away the pink dress and slipped into the beautiful red velvet. Grandma helped her with the pearls while Mamma just watched. Winnie saw those tears again but this time they were in Mamma's eyes.

"Hurry up, Winnie." Howard called. "Some of us want to be on time you know!"

Winnie buckled her shoes and was about to run after Howard, when Uncle Will appeared in the doorway. "You might need these to ring at the end of your poem, Winnie," he said.

Uncle Will had found some old brass bells hanging in the barn and had polished them until they shone like gold. He had tied them with cord so they would be easy for Winnie to ring. Winnie was overwhelmed but she had no time to say anything, for Howard was not waiting another minute. She gave Uncle Will a quick hug, grabbed her grey cloth coat and the bells and ran across the road after Howard.

The Orange Hall glowed. The biggest Christmas tree Winnie had ever seen stood in the corner. It glistened with tinsel and beautiful balls. A large golden star hung at the very top. The ivy garlands were scalloped around the room with big red bows at every other loop. The stage was set with a table and props for the "Cratchett's Family Christmas" play. The little cradle was centre stage with fresh, clean straw inside and out awaiting the baby Jesus. Willa Burbridge, one of the older girls, was already at the piano playing Christmas carols softly as the people were arriving. Winnie was breathless. How was she ever going to get up in front of everyone?

The concert went off without a hitch. The angel choir sang beautifully.

O little town of Bethlehem,
How still we see thee lie;
Above thy deep and dreamless sleep
The silent stars go by…

The "Cratchett's Family Christmas" play brought people to their feet with clapping. Then it was Winnie's turn. Her stomach felt like the inside of Mamma's washing machine when she was doing the laundry. Her head felt thick and her hands were wet and clammy.

"Oh," Winnie panicked, "what if I can't do this after all?"

Just then Winnie felt a strong, gentle hand touch her shoulder. She turned and looked up at her father. "You're fine, Winnie. Go ahead now."

Winnie felt ready. She picked up the bells that Uncle Will had given her and went forward onto the stage. In a clear, heavenly voice Winnie recited the poem that Daddy had written for her.

"The Ringing of the Bells"

In the little town of Bethlehem
A long time ago,
A little girl was restless,
She heard confusion down below.

To her little bed she'd gone
In early eventide,
Her head filled with thoughts
Of hills, where shepherds abide.

Her sleep was soon disturbed
By the ringing of a bell.
Her curious mind wondered
What story it would tell.

Arising from her bed
Out her window she did peek.
Her pounding heart and curious eyes
An answer did seek.

Below her on the street
Was a donkey proud and strong,
A woman on his back
A man walking along.

They went into a stable
With animals around,
She saw a little calf
And heard a bleating sound.

Up in the sky a bright star shone
It filled the hills with light.
Shepherds were descending
To the little stable sight.

Suddenly an angel choir
Appeared up in the sky,
Singing glory to our Saviour
And to our God on high.

The little girl could not believe
Before her very eyes,
A newborn babe appeared
With tiny little cries.

She saw the woman and the man
Kneel down before the manger.
She knew in her heart
There was no fear of danger.

The brightest star she'd ever seen
Shone down upon the stable.
From the east came three men
Their bodies draped in sable.

This was no ordinary child
Her heart was filled with awe.
Before her was the baby
Prophets predicted in the Law.

Once again, she heard the ringing
Of the bells out in the street.
She knew this was a story
For years she would repeat.

Winnie felt calm. And her voice didn't quiver even once. At the end of her recitation she rang the bells. There was a silent awe over the entire hall. Winnie looked out at the people. Suddenly someone from the back of the hall began to clap. And before long the whole place broke into thunderous applause. Winnie's heart was so full. She looked down at her father and his face was beaming. Winnie had tears in her eyes but in her heart she felt she was part of the angel choir.

"Winnie's School Days"
SS # 1 Oakley, Vankoughnet, Muskoka, circa 1950's

"MAGNIFYING GLASSES"

Winnie felt the gravel between her teeth. Her lip was hurting and blood was oozing from her knee. "Winnie," Kyle her older brother exclaimed, "can't you ever watch where you are going?"

Winnie had tripped on a big root of the pine tree at the side of her house and had fallen face first onto the gravel path. Winnie struggled to hold back the tears. Not only did her lip hurt and her knee was bleeding, but her breath was coming in short little gasps. Winnie had "winded herself" as Grandma would say.

This wasn't the first fall Winnie had recently had. Why, in fact, it seemed to Winnie falling was becoming an everyday occurrence.

Grandma had found the Ozonol in the cupboard, put a blob on Winnie's knee, along with a Band-Aid, washed her face with a warm cloth and said, "There you go, Winnie, good as new."

Winnie didn't feel as good as new. In fact she felt so frustrated with herself and she was tired of everyone thinking that she was clumsy. Why just this very morning she wasn't watching where she was going and she bumped right into Trent Mingey on the way to school. He was hanging over the bridge and Winnie, well, she was daydreaming as she was walking along and didn't actually see him. She almost knocked him right into the river!

"Winnie," he snarled, "watch where you are going! You'd walk into a brick wall and not even see it. I think you need magnifying glasses."

"Winnie, don't hold that book so close to your face," Mrs. Hall, Winnie's teacher said to her at school that day. "You're going to ruin your eyesight."

Winnie loved to read. It was the most comforting time of Winnie's day if she could get into a good book and lose herself in the story. The Merriweather Girls, Nancy Drew, and Mimi were some of Winnie's favourites. She loved the excitement and adventure in their lives and pretended she had similar experiences. Winnie tried holding the book back from her face but when she did the words became blurry.

"What's wrong with Mrs. Hall?" Winnie pondered. "Doesn't she realize that you have to hold the book close or you can't see the words?" Winnie waited until Mrs. Hall moved on to another pupil and then slowly edged the book close again.

"You're the teacher's pet!" chided Trent Mingey.

"I am not!" retorted Winnie emphatically.

"You are too!" continued Trent. "You always sit in the front seat closest to Mrs. Hall."

Winnie stopped cold. She hadn't really thought about that before. For once in his life Trent Mingey, who lived across the road from Winnie in the little village of Mistymeadow, was right. Winnie did always scramble to get a seat right at the front of the room.

"But it doesn't have anything to do with being close to Mrs. Hall," Winnie comforted herself. "It's just that I can see the blackboard better from there."

At recess that day, some of the older children wanted to play Red Rover. Willa Burbridge said that she'd be captain of one team and Barnett Moriarty could be captain of the other. Winnie stood waiting as one by one the teams were chosen. Willa called out Brandon, one of Winnie's older brothers, and Marlin Mingey was chosen for Barnett's team. Then Willa selected Tommy Brant and Tina Mae, and Barnett chose Winnie's brothers Kyle and Nathan. On it went right down to where the only ones left were Trent Mingey and Winnie. Winnie was hoping to be on Willa's team because Willa was tall and strong and Winnie knew that she could roar right through the other Red Rover team's line-up. Winnie and Trent were the youngest ones allowed to play Red Rover. Mary Beth, Winnie's little sister, and the other smaller children were off in a corner of the schoolyard playing touch-tag.

Finally Willa called out, "I'll take Trent, and Winnie you can go with Barnett." Winnie scampered over to join her team. Soon the two factions had joined arms at opposite ends of the field.

With arms firmly locked in place, Willa called out "Red Rover, Red Rover, let Winnie come over."

Winnie knew they always called the weakest person to come over first, knowing he or she wouldn't have the strength to run across the field and break through the line-up. Winnie felt a little put out that she would be considered the weakest one on her team. If she could break through the line of the opposing team, she would remain on her own team; if not, she would become part of the opposing team.

Winnie felt the determination soaring inside her. "I'll try to break through Trent and Tina Mae. They appear to be the weakest link."

Winnie took a deep breath. "Run like the wind, Winnie!" She could hear Kyle calling out.

Winnie dug her feet into the ground. She pulled herself up to be as tall and strong as she possibly could. Then she took off.

"Go! Winnie! Run faster! Harder! Winnie, run! Run!" The voices of her team members were ringing in Winnie's ears.

Winnie felt like she was running as she'd never run before. Harder and harder she pushed herself. Trent and Tina Mae were getting closer and closer to her. She was going to break through. She knew that she could do this. Winnie put on one last burst of speed and with all her strength she hit the line. At that precise moment the opposing team shifted a little to the left and, instead of confronting Tina Mae and Trent, Winnie hit a "brick wall," straight into Tommy Brant, the biggest boy in the grade eight class. Winnie crashed to the ground! No more voices, no more cheering, the world went silent! Winnie was out cold!

The next thing Winnie knew, Mrs. Hall was tapping her cheeks. "Come on, Winnie, wake up! Winnie, wake up!"

Winnie opened her eyes. The entire school including her little sister, Mary Beth, with her big worried eyes, was looking down at Winnie. Even Trent Mingey looked a little taken aback.

"What happened?" Winnie asked as Mrs. Hall helped her stand up.

"Winnie," Mrs. Hall said, "you are no match for those big kids! You could have been seriously injured!"

"I am seriously injured," thought Winnie. "My pride is anyway. Everyone is going to think that I am a weakling."

"You ran right into Tommy Brant, Winnie," Mrs. Hall continued. "Didn't you see him there?"

Winnie thought there was no use in explaining that the whole team had shifted to the left causing her to lose her way. No one would believe her anyway.

Recess was over. Winnie sat in her seat but she could not concentrate on anything that Mrs. Hall was saying. Her head hurt and her heart felt as if someone was sitting on it. The map of the world was rolled down and Mrs. Hall was showing the children the different continents: Asia, Africa, Australia and on it went. Winnie didn't need a map. Her head felt as if it was already swirling around the world. Winnie just wanted to go home.

"Mrs. Hall," Winnie approached her teacher, "may I please go home?"

"Are you still not feeling well?" Mrs. Hall queried.

"My head hurts," Winnie responded.

"You may go home," Mrs. Hall agreed, "but Nathan must go with you to make certain that you are all right."

It didn't take Nathan long to jump from his seat. He couldn't believe his good luck at leaving school early. Two or three other children offered to go along as well in case they were needed. But Mrs. Hall assured them that Nathan would do just fine.

Grandma tucked Winnie into bed that night. "It hasn't been your best ever day today, has it?" she asked in a comforting voice. "Why you bumped your lip and skinned your knee, had a confrontation with Trent Mingey and then, if that wasn't enough, you knocked yourself out."

Winnie didn't really need to be reminded about all these things. "Grandma," Winnie queried, "do you think I was just born clumsy?"

"Whatever do you mean, Winnie?" Grandma responded.

"I seem to trip over things and bump into things and fall on my face more times than anyone else," Winnie explained. "Trent Mingey says I need magnifying glasses on my eyes," Winnie continued.

Grandma stopped what she was doing and looked straight at Winnie, right into Winnie's brown eyes for what seemed a long time. "What is she thinking about?" Winnie wondered. But Grandma didn't explain. She just tucked Winnie into bed, gave her a big hug and turned out the light.

The next morning, Winnie's dad came into her room early. Usually he had gone to work by the time Winnie and Mary Beth arose. "What's this I hear about you falling and bumping into things, Winnie?"

Winnie told him about the root of the pine tree and then about almost knocking Trent Mingey into the river, and then she told him about the Red Rover game and how she couldn't really remember anything after reaching the other team.

"We'll have to talk about this some more when I get home from work tonight, Winnie," her dad said. Winnie wondered what this was about. It wasn't as though she'd done anything wrong.

As he turned to go out the door he looked back at Winnie, "You be careful today, Winnie, and watch where you are going!"

Winnie was particularly cautious that day. The next few days came and went and Winnie didn't hear anything further about her clumsiness. She figured that her dad had too many other things on his mind to be worrying about her. Her father owned a lumber mill and he worked long, hard days. The logs had to be cut into lumber and piled in the lumberyard. Then the lumber was scaled, tallied and shipped to places all over the world.

"Winnie!" Mamma called from the kitchen. "Can you come and tell me what the date is on the calendar?"

Winnie came running but wondering all the time why Mamma couldn't read it for herself. Mamma had been a schoolteacher before she married Winnie's dad and she was very clever. Winnie's Uncle Cecil said, "If anyone could make someone learn something, Mamma could."

"Winnie, stand back here beside me." Mamma motioned to Winnie to come around the far side of the table. "Now tell me the date on the calendar from here, Winnie."

Winnie wondered why Mamma was doing this. No one could possibly read the numbers from way back here! Mamma asked Grandma, who was standing nearby, to flip the calendar over to a different month. "Now, Winnie, can you tell me what month that is?" Winnie knew the months of the year off by heart but of course she couldn't see from this far away what the letters said.

"Is this a game, Mamma?" Winnie asked, still wondering what Mamma was getting at.

"No, Winnie dear, this is not a game," Mamma replied. "Your dad and Grandma and I have been wondering lately if you have difficulty seeing properly. I spoke with Mrs. Hall today and she has the same concern."

Winnie didn't want to hear this. Just because she was a little bit clumsy, and because she liked to read with her book close to her face, didn't mean there was something wrong with her.

"Winnie," Mamma continued, "we are going to go to the city and stay with Aunt Lucy and Uncle Alan for a couple of days. While we are there we will take you to Dr. Meighan to have your eyes checked."

Winnie was horrified! Trent Mingey was right. She would be wearing big magnifying glasses on her eyes. Winnie felt this was a conspiracy. Even Grandma, who always took Winnie's side, was in on it.

Winnie moped about the house. "One more day before the eye doctor." She could hear it all now: "Four eyes. Fish eyes. Pollywog eyes." Trent Mingey would be in his glory. And Winnie, well, Winnie would be ruined for life.

"Winnie, whatever is your problem?" Grandma asked as she noticed Winnie lethargically moving about the house. Winnie's despair was so deep she felt even Grandma wouldn't understand.

The next day Winnie and her mother and father arrived at Aunt Lucy and Uncle Alan's. Under other circumstances Winnie would be thrilled to be there. They lived in a pretty house with a stained glass window on either side of the fireplace. And they had blinds on their other windows made from little slats that twisted up and down when you pulled a chord. They also had a television, but when Winnie tried to watch it the picture wasn't clear.

Aunt Lucy was a really good cook. She had made a big meal including a dish she called "Harvard beets." Usually Winnie loved to eat Aunt Lucy's food, but today for some reason she was not hungry.

"Well, what you don't eat for supper, Winnie, we'll save and give you for breakfast," Uncle Alan chided. Winnie didn't know whether to take him seriously or not.

Dr. Meighan's office was very plain: three grey chairs and a table with magazines on it. Winnie hoped no one, not even Mamma, would speak to her until this ordeal was over. Just then a lady with a pleasant face, who Winnie would later find out was Dr. Meighan's wife, came out where Winnie was waiting and called her in.

"Go ahead, Winnie," her dad prodded. "We'll be right here."

"Right here!" The anxiousness sounded in Winnie's voice. "Aren't you and Mamma coming in with me?"

Mamma, recognizing Winnie's uneasiness, stepped up. "I'll go in with you, Winnie."

Once inside, Dr. Meighan slid a machine with big round rings in front of Winnie's eyes. "Read these letters for me, Winnie."

Winnie started with the biggest letter. "E" she said. Then she went on to "F, G, M," then to the third line, "P, O, L." All the time Dr. Meighan was changing a little switch on the side of the black rings and each time he did so Winnie could read another line a little further along.

"That's fine, Winnie," he said. "Now I am going to look in your eyes with a bright light. You look straight ahead and this will only take a minute."

Winnie felt herself begin to relax, just a little. As Dr. Meighan completed his examination Winnie ventured forth with the question that had been on her mind from the very beginning.

"Dr. Meighan?" she asked.

"Yes, Winnie," he responded.

"Will I have to wear magnifying glasses on my eyes?"

A slight grin showed at the corners of Dr. Meighan's mouth but he spoke in a very serious manner. "Winnie, you do need glasses, most definitely, but, no, they will not be magnifying glasses. You are near-sighted, Winnie. That means you have difficulty seeing anything that is very far away from you. But with proper glasses you will be just fine."

The sense of relief Winnie felt was huge as she scampered out of the chair. She waited while Mamma and Daddy spoke with the lady at the desk and discovered that the glasses would arrive by mail at Winnie's home in about two weeks.

The two weeks passed quickly. One day, a Friday it was, Winnie's dad arrived home from a trip into town. "Your parcel's here, Winnie," he called from the kitchen door. Winnie didn't know whether to be excited or not.

"Open it, Winnie," Mary Beth encouraged. Winnie opened the parcel and there in their very own perfect, little case was a small pair of pretty pink glasses.

"Wow, Winnie!" Mary Beth exclaimed. "Can I try them on?" But Winnie wouldn't let them out of her grasp. She ran upstairs to her room. Very gently she removed them from the case and put them on her nose.

Suddenly, Winnie's world changed. The books on the shelf had titles Winnie could read. There were little dust balls in the corner of her room that Winnie couldn't believe were there before. Even the colour of her clothes seemed different. Then just as she caught a glimpse of herself in the mirror on the dresser, Mary Beth came into the room. "Oh, Winnie, you look beautiful!" Mary Beth exclaimed.

Winnie couldn't help but smile at her reflection. For the first time ever, she felt she saw what she really looked like. Her glasses were small and transparent pink and hardly showed on her face at all. It wasn't the glasses she noticed so much as it was seeing what she looked like and especially how brown her eyes were.

Hand in hand Mary Beth and Winnie descended the staircase. Practically everyone in the family was there awaiting Winnie's reaction. Her little brother Evan's skin looked soft and pink. Brandon had freckles. Winnie hadn't noticed that before. Kyle's dark eyes sparkled more than Winnie ever remembered. And Nathan smiled at her with his quiet grin. The world had come alive for Winnie.

She ran from room to room looking at every detail. Mamma's china dishes had tiny flowers on them and the numbers on the clock looked big and bold. Winnie ran to the kitchen and from the far side of the table she could read the month and day on the calendar. Then she went outside. Why Winnie could see right over to the Mingey's house. She could even see Trent and Marlin playing catch in the front yard and Mrs. Mingey hanging clothes on the wash-line. Winnie's world had come into focus. The grass was greener, the sky was bluer and even the animals looked more alert. Winnie was overwhelmed!

Grandma tucked Winnie into bed that night. "Sometimes we don't even know things need to change, do we Grandma?" Winnie asked.

"That's true, Winnie," Grandma responded. "Sometimes we need others to recognize the necessity for change in us and all we must do is accept it."

Winnie gently placed her new glasses in their case and laid it on the nightstand and went to sleep.

Trent Mingey was waiting at Winnie's house early the next morning. "Are you ready to come and stumble through another day?" Trent wheedled.

Winnie didn't even respond. She felt a new strength and a new confidence within herself. She held her head high and walked to school. The world around her was crisp and clear but what was even more amazing to Winnie was that Trent Mingey didn't even notice her new glasses.

"The Gathering Place"
St. David's Presbyterian Church, Vankoughnet, Muskoka, circa 1950's

"A WHAT?"

Winnie tugged at her socks. No matter how hard she tried, she could not cover the mole on her right leg. "These socks are too short," Winnie exclaimed, "and I'm not wearing them!" Mamma had just bought them for Winnie when she and Winnie's dad had gone to town on Saturday.

"Whatever are you talking about, Winnie?" Mamma asked. "I'm certain I bought the right size for you. Now just put them on and we'll be on our way. Everyone is waiting!"

It was Sunday morning. Winnie, along with all her family, including Grandma and Uncle Cecil and Uncle Will, was on her way to church. There were so many in her family they couldn't all go in the same vehicle. Usually Winnie's dad would drive the car and take Grandma and Mamma and the little kids, Winnie, Mary Beth and Evan, while Uncle Will took the big old Fargo log truck with Uncle Cecil inside and Winnie's older brothers, Howard, Brandon, Kyle and Nathan, riding on the back. When Hope was home from the city for the weekend she got to ride in the car as well.

Grandma said, "When a young woman lives in the city she can't be riding in a dusty truck on the weekends." But Hope never seemed to mind if she had to take a turn in the truck. Winnie begged to have a turn but her dad only gave in if two of the bigger boys would be one on either side of her.

Winnie liked going to church. She and Mary Beth and Evan would sit with Winnie's dad and Grandma while Mamma went up to the front to play the organ. The organ required all of Mamma's concentration because she needed to use her feet to pump the pedals and her fingers to play the music. Once in a while Evan would escape

Daddy's grasp and run up to Mamma. Winnie's dad would calmly go and retrieve him. He seemed to understand that Evan, like Winnie, found it difficult to sit still.

Winnie sat as quietly as possible. Mamma was playing softly on the organ. Winnie recognized the tune. It was called "In the Garden." Sometimes at home Mamma and Daddy would sit side by side at the piano and Mamma would play and they both would sing:

I come to the garden alone
While the dew is still on the roses…

Winnie thought that was their favourite hymn.

Winnie felt herself beginning to wiggle. The minister's voice was a bit of a hum to Winnie. She tried to concentrate on what he was saying but the most she could think about was that he had an unusual hair-do. She wondered if it was really his own hair or was it one of those wigs, Hope had told them about, that men in the city sometimes wore. She must remember to ask Hope when she came home next time. Suddenly everyone was standing and they were singing,

"Yes, we'll gather at the river,
The beautiful, the beautiful river…

Winnie supposed they meant the river that ran through her village but she couldn't for the life of her think why they were all going to gather there.

Mr. Mingey, who lived across the road from Winnie, passed around the offering plate. Winnie didn't put in anything as she had left the money Uncle Cecil had given her on the kitchen table at home. She caught Howard's glance out of the corner of her eye. He was her oldest brother and felt it necessary to remind Winnie from time to time that she'd forget her head if it wasn't attached. Winnie looked down. Mary Beth popped her offering right into the plate. The minister said "Amen" and everyone headed for the back of the church.

"What's on your leg, Winnie?" Trent Mingey asked with a big smirk on his face as Winnie came out of church. "It looks like a fly landed there!"

Winnie wanted to give him a big push. Trent knew it was a mole on her leg and he also knew Winnie was self-conscious about it.

"You look like someone hit you with a frying pan!" Winnie retorted. She knew she had to retaliate quickly or the teasing would continue and Trent Mingey would think he had won.

"What's going on, Winnie?" Mamma asked as she noticed Winnie and the neighbour boy in a not so pleasant conversation.

"Nothing" they both said and retreated each to their own family.

Winnie was disgruntled. Things weren't going so well in her life right now. She had the "mole". Oh, how Winnie hated that word. There it was right on her leg and the new socks Mamma had bought weren't long enough to cover it up. Trent Mingey was teasing her constantly about something. This didn't bother Winnie as a rule because she knew she could give it right back, if necessary. But lately, there were other things on Winnie's mind. She was having difficulty determining just what it was that was bothering her.

"Maybe it isn't just one thing," Winnie thought to herself. "Maybe it's a lot of things all jumbled together."

Hope had just recently moved to the big city to work and so only came home every other weekend. Winnie missed Hope. She was always there for Winnie and stuck up for her when her older brothers teased her. Winnie felt that while she could take on Trent Mingey, she was no match for her brothers. So instead of fighting back, she retreated to the bathroom.

"It's the only room in the house where one gets a little privacy," Uncle Will had said one day, when he was tired of her brothers asking him to do things.

"Winnie, you seem to be at loose ends," Mamma said as Winnie wandered around the house. "Can't you find something of interest to do with your time? Perhaps Grandma has some vegetables you can pick in the garden," Mamma continued.

Winnie's step immediately quickened. She straightened her clothes, washed her face and brushed her hair. Gardening wasn't part of her agenda for the day. She had better look alive and find something to do or Mamma would insist on her plan.

Just then Ranger, the family dog, began barking. "Someone must be coming," Mamma called out. "See who it is, Winnie."

Winnie, relieved to have gardening off Mamma's mind, ran to the window. Much to her amazement a car without any top had driven into the yard and even more startling to Winnie, Hope was in the car.

"Mamma!" Winnie exclaimed. "Come quick. Hope's home and some man is helping her out of a car with no top!"

Mamma, who had been baking pies, came running in from the kitchen wiping her hands on her apron. "Who is he?" Mamma queried. "And what's he doing without a shirt?"

Winnie explained, "It's not the man who has no top; it's the car!"

Mamma stood beside Winnie and they both watched in amazement as a dark haired young man closed the car door behind Hope.

Winnie's day was definitely looking up. "Mary Beth! Evan! Come quick! Hope's bringing home a stranger," Winnie called out in excitement.

As they came running, all three raced to the door to let Hope in. Hope hugged them all but she had kind of a "sheepish look," as Grandma would call it, on her face as she looked at Mamma.

"Mamma," Hope spoke in her soft voice, "I'd like you to meet Christos." He picked me up at the train station when I arrived home from the city. He's going to be our new minister at the church for the summer."

Mamma was very quiet. She didn't speak for what Winnie thought was a very long time. Suddenly she thrust out her hand to Christos and said, "It's nice to meet you. Welcome to our home."

Winnie was bursting. She wanted to be the first to tell her brothers that Hope had brought home a young man and somebody even Mamma hadn't seen before. Just then Winnie felt herself being guided into the corner of the room and realized it was Hope's hand on her shoulder.

"Don't you jump to any conclusions here, Winnie!" Hope whispered. "Christos just happened to be at the train station when I got off the train and he gave me a ride home." Winnie didn't know what was behind Hope's explanation but she knew it wouldn't stop her from telling her brothers.

The whole house was abuzz. Winnie's brothers were impressing Christos with their ability to throw a football. Winnie and Mary Beth were atwitter with telling Uncle Cecil and Uncle Will that Hope had come home with a stranger. Mamma and Grandma were busy in the kitchen preparing supper. Winnie's dad was unusually quiet.

Then the bomb dropped. Christos asked Winnie's dad if he could take Hope out on a date. "No one in the house had ever gone on a date," Winnie thought. "Daddy is bound to say no."

The room was suspended in silence. Winnie looked from face to face but no one was moving. Hope had no colour in her face. "Totally white," Winnie thought. Daddy cleared his throat, which was always a sign that something important was coming.

"Thank you for asking my permission, Christos. But I think the person you really need to ask is Hope herself. If Hope feels you are someone she wants to spend time with then that's good enough for me." Winnie watched as Christos looked at Hope and Hope's face went from white to red.

"You two run along now and go for a walk to the river," Mamma broke the silence. Hope and Christos attempted to make their escape as Brandon and Kyle and Nathan moved to follow along.

"Just a minute," Mamma said. "There are chores to be done. You boys had better get busy." Great groans were heard from the boys as Hope and Christos walked off alone.

Winnie's restlessness had subsided for a while but as evening wore on she began to feel her agitation return. "Winnie, what can I do to settle you down?" Grandma queried as she watched Winnie moving from place to place inside and outside the house.

"Grandma," Winnie said, "why does everything have to change? Why can't things just stay the same?"

"Whatever do you mean, Winnie?" Grandma responded.

"Why does Hope have to go away to work and not live here with us anymore? And what if someday she meets a young man like Christos and gets married and goes far away from all of us? And what if my mole gets so big it takes over my whole leg?" Winnie was on a roll with one question after another.

"Winnie, Winnie, Winnie," Grandma exclaimed. "Slow down! I can't answer so many questions all at once. For one thing, Winnie, life changes for every one of us. That's what life is all about and, secondly, there will always be things in life that worry us, or that we think aren't perfect – like the mole on your leg. But the changes and the worries aren't necessarily bad things. Sometimes they turn out better than we ever expected. And you know Winnie, I think that mole on your leg is a beauty mark."

"A what?" Winnie exclaimed.

"A beauty mark," Grandma continued. "It's a part of you that makes you special and beautiful."

Winnie looked down at her leg and immediately reached down and rolled her socks down to her ankles. Never in her wildest dreams had she thought of her mole as a beauty mark. This was definitely something new to ponder. Winnie's restlessness started to go away. She snuggled up to Grandma and they both sat in silence for a little while. Then Winnie with her brown eyes wide open looked up at Grandma.

"Thank you, Grandma," she said.

The next morning Winnie skipped off to school without any socks on at all. Barely outside her driveway she met Trent Mingey waiting for her. "Hey, Winnie, why no cover-up today?" he asked mockingly. "I can see your mole and I think it is getting bigger."

"It's not a mole," Winnie said indignantly and stuck her nose in the air.

"Yeah, well, what is it then?" retorted Trent.

Winnie in her most defiant manner looked down her nose at him and said, "It's a beauty mark!" Then she turned and walked to school leaving Trent Mingey feeling very much put in his place.

"The Fall Fair"
Bracebridge, Muskoka, circa 1950's

"UNRESOLVED ISSUES"

"Left, right, left, left, right," Winnie concentrated as hard as she could.

"You're a little out of step, Winnie," Mrs. Hall, her teacher called out.

Winnie looked down at her feet willing them to move in alternating fashion in step with the other children.

"She can't help it," chimed in Trent Mingey. "Both her feet are left ones."

It was the week before the Fall Fair. Everyone in Winnie's school, S. S. # 1 Oak Leaf, was practising. They were to march as an entire school along with children from schools all over the district of Pusquaka in a big parade through the streets of Silver Bridge on the day of the Fair.

Winnie lived in the little village of Mistymeadow about thirty miles from Silver Bridge. Each year when the Fall Fair came to town Winnie and her family would go. Mamma would pack a big picnic lunch. Winnie's dad would declare a holiday from work so everyone who worked for him at his lumber mill would have the day free to go too.

Uncle Will drove the old Fargo log truck and the older boys, Brandon, Kyle and Nathan, rode on the back while Uncle Cecil rode along inside. Winnie's dad would take the car and Mamma and the little kids, Winnie, Mary Beth and Evan, went along with him. Arrangements would be made for everyone to meet at noon for the picnic lunch.

Winnie tossed and turned. She couldn't sleep at night. Her brain was in a turmoil. "Left, left, right, right, left,…" over and over it went in her mind. How would she ever get it straight?

She wanted so badly to perform well in the parade but her feet just weren't cooperating. She knew she wasn't clumsy anymore because now she had new glasses and she could see perfectly. Why just today in school, Mrs. Hall had asked her to stand at the back of the room and read from the blackboard the names of all the children, while she lined them up in twos in preparation for the parade. Kyle, Winnie's brother and Jimmie Brant would carry the banner. Winnie and her classmates had collected real oak leaves and waxed them and put them on the banner. Tina Mae and Marjie, two of the older girls, did the lettering. Winnie thought it looked beautiful: "Mistymeadow Public School S.S. # 1 Oak Leaf."

"Come on, children, line up, now." Mrs. Hall tried to get their attention. "Call out the next names, Winnie."

"Audrey and Tina Mae, Mary and Jeanette, Bart and Nathan," and on it went. Winnie just knew that she'd have to march beside Trent Mingey. Maybe just this once Mrs. Hall would let her and Mary Beth be together and Trent and Mona Hall would march side by side.

Winnie could hardly believe it was already fall. The summer had gone so quickly. Her friends Beryl and Mandy had been gone back to the city for two weeks. They had visited along with their families at their grandmother's place on the other side of the Misty River for the entire summer.

"Winnie, are you paying attention?" Mrs. Hall's voice startled her. Winnie's mind came back to the task at hand.

"Mrs. Hall," she enquired, "could Mary Beth and I march together in the parade?" Mrs. Hall didn't answer Winnie immediately. Winnie, thinking Mrs. Hall hadn't heard her clearly, called out a little louder, "Excuse me, Mrs. Hall, but could Mary Beth and I march together this time?"

This was only Mary Beth's second time to be in the Fall Fair parade and Winnie felt that on that basis alone they should be allowed to be together. "Mamma wouldn't want Mary Beth to get separated from the other children," Winnie continued.

Mrs. Hall, looking somewhat exasperated, replied, "Just read the list the way it is on the board, Winnie. If there are to be any changes I'll be the one to make them!" Winnie saw the smirk on Trent Mingey's face. She'd give anything to wipe that off she thought to herself.

Winnie's thoughts drifted back again to the summer. Winnie had some unresolved issues. Ever since Ranger, the family dog, had died, Winnie felt nervous when anyone went away from home. She couldn't really admit this to anyone for fear they'd think she was silly. She hated having to say goodbye to her friends Beryl and Mandy knowing that it would be a whole year before she'd see them again. And although her older sister, Hope, who worked in the city came home every other weekend, Winnie still felt sad when Hope got on the train on Sunday night.

"All right, Winnie, step up here in line, now," Mrs. Hall called to her. "I think because of your heights," she continued, "that you and Trent should march together and Mary Beth and Mona can bring up the rear."

Trent Mingey was the same age as Winnie and he lived across the road from her. He loved to tease and Winnie could hear him chuckling under his breath and saying, "Right, left, left, uh, or is it right?" in a low, muffled voice. Winnie knew that this was solely to irritate her.

It was the day before the Fair. Mamma had made matching green corduroy skirts for Winnie and Mary Beth to wear in the parade. "Dark skirts and pants and white blouses and shirts," Mrs. Hall had said.

Brandon, Winnie's older brother had just begun high school two weeks before. He arrived home on the school bus filled with excitement. He told of the big trucks rolling into Silver Bridge with all kinds of equipment on them. He and Marlin Mingey had gone to the fair grounds over the noon hour.

"There is a Ferris wheel a hundred feet high in the sky!" he exclaimed. "And swings that with centrifugal force go so far out your face is parallel with the ground," he reported excitedly. "And Winnie and Mary Beth and Evan can go on the merry-go-round. It has beautiful carousel horses painted in blue and pink and yellow with manes and tails in white and black and brown." "The wildest ride of all," he continued, "is the giant roller coaster. Kyle and Nathan and I can try that one."

Winnie was thrilled to hear about the "midway" as Grandma called it with all its different rides, but she felt that although the merry-go-round sounded attractive, she definitely planned to try out the roller coaster.

Fall Fair day dawned cool and sunny. Winnie and Mary Beth squeezed together in an attempt to see themselves in the mirror at the same time. "Oh, Mary Beth, don't we look great?" Winnie giggled at her sister. Mary Beth looked a little shy and nodded her head.

Many of the schools were already lining up as Winnie and her sister and brothers arrived. "Over here, children," Mrs. Hall called out as she saw them entering the park. Quickly they joined the line in their assigned spots.

"Now, remember," Mrs. Hall continued, "when the band begins to play be ready to lift your left foot all at the same time."

Winnie was concentrating. "Begin with my left, begin with my left," over and over she said in her mind.

Her school really looked smart, Winnie thought to herself. With our dark skirts and pants and white shirts we look just like we're wearing uniforms. Winnie had often thought that wearing a uniform every day to school would be a good idea. Why she could just put on the same clothes two or three days in a row and nobody would know the difference.

Suddenly the band began: "Ta boom! Ta boom! Ta boom! Boom! Boom!" Winnie jumped and her right foot shot up involuntarily. They were on their way.

"You're supposed to start with your left foot, Winnie," Trent Mingey snarled.

Winnie did a little two-step trying her best to get in time with everyone else. "Left, right, left, right." Her head was spinning. There was no doubt Winnie was off on the wrong foot.

"Right, left, left, right," she struggled to get into step. She looked over at Trent Mingey trying to watch his feet and follow along.

Winnie didn't hear the band stop. She was so busy keeping her feet marching. She also didn't notice that everyone had paused. Winnie kept marching, "left, right, left, right, right," right into Bart Bonway. Bart was marching beside Nathan and, although he was strong, he wasn't particularly tall. Winnie caught him right off guard.

"It was a domino effect," Winnie's Uncle Will explained later. Winnie into Bart, Bart into Mary Brant, Mary into Audrey, and on it went right up the line to Kyle and Jimmie Brant. Well, needless to say, the waxed oak leaves flew right off the banner. And the banner itself went flying right into Gruffington School S.S. # 1 Scraper and the "domino effect" continued.

Winnie wanted to wake up. "Please, let this be a dream," she begged within herself.

But this was no dream! Children were scrambling everywhere to re-establish their proper positions. Winnie was back in line but Trent Mingey was no longer marching beside her. He had changed places of his own accord with Mary Beth saying he'd prefer the safety of marching beside Mona Hall.

"You're a walking war zone, Winnie," he exclaimed.

Winnie felt Mary Beth's little hand snuggle itself in hers and together they marched hand in hand through the streets of Silver Bridge and right into the fair grounds.

Mamma and Daddy and Evan were waiting for Winnie and Mary Beth and the older boys when they arrived at the fair grounds. Kyle and Nathan quickly reported in, asked for some spending money, and got out of there as quickly as possible. "Do something about her," they said in passing. Winnie felt devastated.

The Fall Fair itself was everything and more than Winnie had imagined. "Come along," she heard her father's voice calling.

The Ferris wheel was spinning round and round with people in seats high in the air laughing and squealing with delight. The roller coaster, called "The Wild One," zoomed past Winnie at an enormous speed. "Swoosh." Winnie stood back and caught her breath. The midway was alive with colour and movement and music. A calliope went rolling by. Winnie's eyes were as big as saucers.

"It sounds like an entire band is inside the machine," she spoke out to anyone who was listening. A man dressed in a top hat and striped shirt and bright red suspenders was driving it. A cute little monkey sat on his shoulder. Winnie was fascinated. "Look, Mary Beth, the monkey is looking right at us."

Mary Beth didn't respond but Winnie was so enthralled with the sights and sounds she didn't pay any attention. There were booths set up everywhere. People were throwing balls at markers and winning stuffed animals. Winnie thought she would try that. She looked at everything: people, animals, colourful flags. Out of the corner of her eye she noticed two or three of the older boys from her school walking by. They looked over at Winnie and giggled amongst themselves. Suddenly Winnie remembered the episode in the parade and she felt very self-conscious.

She turned back to her family. Where was her family? She looked to the left, then the right, or was it the right and then the left? There were people everywhere. Winnie was confused. "Daddy! Mamma!" she called out. Where were they? "Mary Beth! Evan! Daddy! Mamma!"

Winnie felt a little hysterical. She hadn't gone anywhere. Where had they gone? How could they leave her behind? She vaguely remembered her father calling her but they wouldn't just leave her. Her face was hot and her hands were clammy. Winnie felt a sense of panic rising inside her. She looked around. The Ferris wheel had moved away from her and she was no longer anywhere near the roller coaster. Her family hadn't left her; she had wandered away from them.

Winnie was alone and frightened. Winnie was lost! She felt the tears stinging her eyes. Her body began to shake uncontrollably. People were moving all around her but Winnie didn't see them. The noise of the midway seemed a distant roar. Winnie's whole life was flashing before her. She thought about Mamma and Daddy and all her brothers and sisters and Grandma.

"Oh, Grandma, where are you when I need you? You can find anything when you need to. Oh, Grandma, find me now!" But Winnie knew Grandma hadn't even come to the Fair today. She had said that she'd stay home and do the chores so the rest of the family could have a day out. Winnie was lost forever.

Just then Winnie felt a firm hand on her shoulder. She jumped so hard it made her breath come out in spurts.

"Winnie dear, whatever are you doing here by yourself?"

It was Mrs. Hall's hand on her shoulder. Winnie began to sob. "Oh, Mrs. Hall," she cried, "everything was so exciting and I was so busy watching everything that I must have wandered away from my family. And now I am lost and I probably won't see them ever again."

"Winnie, Winnie, Winnie," Mrs. Hall said in the most comforting voice Winnie had ever heard from her. "Your entire family has spread out through the whole fair grounds along with anyone else they can recruit and they are looking for you. They are so worried, Winnie, and I'm the one lucky enough to find you. Take my hand and we'll go and find your mamma and daddy." Winnie had never loved Mrs. Hall as much as she did right at that moment.

"There she is!" Kyle and Nathan called out simultaneously.

"Oh, Winnie, we thought you were lost forever," Mary Beth chimed in.

Mamma hugged Winnie so hard Winnie thought she couldn't breath. "Thank God you are safe, Winnie!"
Winnie's dad came over and picked her right up in his arms. "Don't ever go off like that again, Winnie. You gave us a terrible fright."

Winnie looked at her dad. She thought she saw tears in his eyes. "I'm sorry, Daddy," she said, "I wasn't paying attention. I didn't even realize I'd wandered away."

Winnie didn't like it when people went away from her but she hadn't thought how others would feel if she were the one to go away. The whole family found their way back to their vehicles and drove safely home.

Winnie was exhausted. That evening as she and Grandma sat on the edge of the bed she related all the events of the day. She told Grandma everything: the parade, the "domino effect", the midway, and mostly she told her about getting lost.

"These things just seem to happen to me. I try harder than anyone else at everything. I feel things others don't feel. I worry about things others don't worry about. I just want to be me." Winnie felt a lot of issues in her life never seemed to get resolved.

"Winnie dear," Grandma said in her gentlest voice, "you live life with an intensity far beyond your years." Winnie listened but she wasn't sure what Grandma was talking about.

"Sometimes, Winnie, you try so hard you defeat yourself. You wanted so badly to march well today that you concentrated totally on the task at hand and completely forgot that you were there to enjoy yourself. As far as being lost is concerned, Winnie," she continued, "you have a wonderful gift of being able to notice details but sometimes you forget to see the whole picture. You were so busy watching the activities in front of you, you neglected to notice you were wandering away from your family."

A little light was beginning to dawn in Winnie's head. "You mean I need to see the whole horse and not just his head?" Winnie asked.

Grandma chuckled. "That might be one way to put it, Winnie. Living in the moment is fine, but the moments need to be connected to one another."

Winnie thought she understood.

"And sometimes, Winnie, we need to let go of our issues and they will eventually resolve themselves."

Winnie sighed and crawled into bed beside Mary Beth. "Thank you Mary Beth for walking with me today and thank you Mrs. Hall for finding me and thank you Grandma," she whispered.

Mary Beth was already asleep. Winnie listened as Grandma began singing softly,

> I once was lost, but now am found;
> Was blind, but now I see.

Winnie knew that was Grandma's favourite hymn. Winnie fell asleep.

"The General Store"
Vankoughnet, Muskoka, circa 1950's

89.

"WHEN DREAMS COME TRUE"

The briskness of the night filtered through Winnie's cloth coat. Her mother had told her to put a sweater underneath but, in her rush not to be left behind, she had neglected to do so. Howard walked so quickly, and if she hesitated even a moment, she found it hard to catch up. Breathing was difficult as she struggled to keep pace with his long strides. Her thin legs were long too, and gangly enough, but Howard was nine years older and finding it difficult not to feel it a nuisance to have Winnie tagging along.

The lights of the General Store shone mistily through the frosted panes as they approached. Even the word "Store" was almost obscured from Winnie's vision. Winnie loved the General Store: the warm blast of air that greeted her as the door opened; the little tinkling bell that hung above the door and announced the arrival of a customer; and the multitude of aromas that taunted her nose as she entered.

It was two weeks till Christmas, but already the store was filled with wonderful things. The big glass jars on the counter held countless numbers of humbugs, jellybeans, liquorice allsorts, and those special chocolates with the pink and white and yellow centres. Row upon row of warm woollen mittens and socks were strung on wire lines high above Winnie's head. Wheels of Cherry Hill cheese with big wedges already cut from them stood in the glass cabinet. In the far corner, behind the box stove, almost every cubbyhole in the Post Office was filled with Christmas mail.

Mr. Hall came from the back room as Winnie and Howard entered the store. He smelled like smoked bacon with a touch of ginger and maybe a little whiff of cinnamon. Winnie liked Mr. Hall. She liked the way he smiled at everyone who came into his store; she liked the old blue and grey striped apron he wore; and she liked the way he always spoke to her as if she were a grown-up. She even liked the way he smelled.

Howard recited to Mr. Hall the list of articles his mother required, marking off each item with a check as they appeared on the counter. Howard always did everything in a business-like manner. He had just returned from college this morning for the holidays, and he seemed more serious about things than ever before, but Winnie guessed that was how people got when they were nine years older.

Howard finished the list and Mr. Hall marked all the articles on the bill. Winnie's eyes danced quickly around the store absorbing all she could before going out in the cold. She would picture it in her mind tonight as she went to sleep. That last glance brought more for Winnie to think about than she had anticipated. There, high on a shelf, sat the most beautiful teddy bear Winnie had ever seen. He was fat and brown and his fur was softly tufted over his body. Around his neck was a shiny red satin bow. His eyes caught Winnie's attention. How had she not seen him before? He was looking directly at her. One eye was open wide; the other appeared to have a slight squint to it.

"Mr. Hall," Winnie exclaimed, "where did that teddy come from?"

Mr. Hall explained that he had ordered it from the city and it had just arrived this afternoon. Winnie had seen teddy bears like this one in the Christmas catalogue, and many times as she hugged her cloth doll that Mamma had made, she pretended it was one of the beautiful bears she had seen on the pages.

Tears came to Winnie's eyes as the cold air bit sharply on her face. A shiver went through her slight body as it adjusted to the temperature change outside. But her heart thumped with excitement at having seen the bear.

"Howard," Winnie hesitantly approached her older brother. "Did you see the new teddy bear on Mr. Hall's shelf?"

"Now, Winnie," Howard seemed to read her thoughts, "don't get any ideas. You know Mamma says you need a new coat, and Mary Beth's leggings already have patches. There won't be money for teddy bears in this family this Christmas!"

Howard was always so practical. He saw things the way they were. Winnie knew he was right, but dreaming helped her soften the edges of reality and that's what she intended to do.

No mention was made of the teddy bear and the days till Christmas became fewer. Mamma was busy sewing a doll for Mary Beth and Winnie enjoyed being in on the secret. She knew little Evan was receiving a quilt for his crib. Grandma had been working on it for months, cutting out pieces from old dresses and sewing them together with great patience. Bit by bit emerged a beautiful masterpiece for Evan's bed. Uncle Will, too, was carving a rattle for Evan that he could hold in his own little hand. Winnie's father was spending many nights in the shed outside the house. She imagined he was making something for her older brothers.

Four more days and Hope would be home. She was the oldest child in the family and a grown-up. Hope worked in the city and even had to work the morning of Christmas Eve. Winnie loved it when Hope came home. She would let Winnie help wrap the presents she had bought in the city and Winnie loved to imagine the shops they had come from. Winnie knew what Hope was getting for Christmas. Grandma had taken her own watch to the watchmaker's and had it cleaned and a new band put on it. This was going to be Hope's present because Grandma said, "Any young woman working in the city needs to be aware of the time."

Winnie hadn't been back to Mr. Hall's store since she had first seen the teddy. Part of her longed to go for another glimpse of him and part of her felt reluctant for fear he was no longer there.

The house seemed quiet to Winnie, considering Christmas was just three days away. Howard left early each morning. He had arranged with Mr. Hall to work for him during the Christmas rush. The other boys, Brandon, Kyle and Nathan, were busy with Winnie's dad and Uncle Will piling the loads of winter wood that the horses and sleigh had drawn to the back door.

Winnie didn't know what to do with herself. She drew some pictures; she read from her book; she watched Grandma working on Evan's quilt. She tried not to think of the teddy, not to let her mind even hope. She knew in her heart there was no money to be spent on a fancy, store-bought teddy. Maybe no one would buy him and she could go into Mr. Hall's store once in a while and just look up at him. Maybe Mr. Hall would even let her hold him sometimes.

"Oh, Winnie, stop thinking about him!" she reprimanded herself.

Winnie pressed her nose against the window. The snowflakes were so big and they looked like the lacy paper ones she had cut out at school last week. Dad and Nathan had been gone for over an hour now. They had taken the truck to town to pick up Hope at the train station. Waiting was hard for Winnie. Mary Beth climbed on a chair beside her and the two of them waited together watching their breath fog the window.

On Christmas Eve the wood floor shone from a fresh coat of wax and the tree in the corner was the best one they had ever had. "A perfect shape," Winnie's dad had said when he set it up.

A long row of stockings hung by the fireplace, each person having chosen the best one he or she had. Winnie and Kyle had made nametags to put on each stocking, so there would be no mistaking whose they were in the morning.

Christmas morning was hardest of all on Winnie's patience. Her mother insisted that they eat a good breakfast and then the Christmas story was read from Grandma's Bible. Finally, when everyone had gathered round the tree, Winnie's dad handed out the gifts. There seemed to be lots of parcels under the tree. Winnie's dad had carved new skis for the older boys. Hope got tears in her eyes when she opened the gift of Grandma's watch; Mary Beth put on her leggings and danced around the room with the doll Mamma had made; and Evan shook his rattle so hard he tired himself out, much to Uncle Will's delight.

Winnie's parcel was bulky and soft and spongy and, when she started to unwrap it, she felt a fuzziness between her fingers. Did she dare look? A quick glance! It was brown! Her heart jumped. Could it be? Her agile fingers pulled off the rest of the paper, and there unfolding before her was a warm brown winter coat. Winnie struggled to keep back the tears. She knew how much she needed that coat. She knew how hard her mother and dad had worked to save the money to buy it. In her head she was thankful; in her heart she longed for the teddy that sat on Mr. Hall's shelf.

Grandma began to clear up the wrappings, folding them tidily in a box, and saving each tag so all could have a good look at one another's gifts.

Howard stooped down and crawled way under the tree. "I think we've forgotten one, Dad," he exclaimed and pulled out a parcel previously hidden from sight. "This one's for Winnie," he said and read the tag: "To Winnie, our little dreamer, Love from Howard."

Winnie's hands trembled as she gently unwrapped the gift. Howard had never before given her anything on his own. What was this? The paper slid from her lap and there sat the teddy from Mr. Hall's store with one eye open wide and the other one squinting a little. Winnie shrieked with delight and surprise! She ran to Howard and threw her arms around him with teddy being squashed between them.

Howard, practical business-like Howard, was the one who always saw things as they were. Beneath this facade beat the heart of a dreamer too, a heart sensitive to the depth of Winnie's longing. She saw the tears well in Howard's eyes and felt his heart surge with joy as he returned her hug.

Howard, dear Howard, had worked hard for Mr. Hall to earn money for the teddy because he had realized the need for Winnie's dream to come true.

"The Parlour"
Bracebridge, Muskoka, circa 1950's

97.

"THE HOMECOMING"

Winnie winced as she tried to drink her hot chocolate. Her tongue was so sore. Earlier she, Mary Beth and Evan had been sleigh riding on the hill at the back of the house. She had stuck her tongue on the icy sleigh and it wouldn't come off. Mary Beth had run for help. Mamma had to put warm water on the sleigh to release Winnie's tongue.

Evan thought all this was very funny and Howard, in his matter of fact way, said, "Well, Winnie, your tongue gets you into trouble one way or another, doesn't it?"

Winnie was annoyed at her brother's remark but this was not the time to comment. Howard had promised to take Winnie into town tonight to see Grandma and she was determined not to say anything that might change his mind.

Grandma had always lived at home with the rest of the family. She belonged there, Winnie felt. But recently Aunt Ann had retired from nursing and moved into an apartment in town. She wanted Grandma to live with her to keep her company.

Winnie missed Grandma a lot. Grandma had always been there for Winnie ever since she could remember. She rubbed Winnie's chest with Raleigh's ointment when she had a cold. She found things for Winnie when Winnie thought they were lost forever. And Grandma always had a hug for Winnie, even when she didn't deserve one.

"Winnie, if you're coming with me, you'd better hurry," Howard called out. He was Winnie's oldest brother and he sometimes got impatient with her. She even heard him telling Mamma once, "That child spends too much time daydreaming and not enough time doing things!"

Winnie gave her teddy bear a hug and scampered to put on her warm brown coat and leggings. This was one time she wouldn't keep Howard waiting. She was excited about seeing Grandma and Aunt Ann, but she was also anticipating her first view of an apartment. Winnie had read about them in books but had never seen one in real life.

The drive into town seemed endless to Winnie. She tried to think of interesting things in her mind so she wouldn't get restless. Howard would accuse her of making him run off the road if she couldn't sit still. Howard was a good driver. He had had his licence for about a year now, but it was only recently that Winnie's dad had allowed him to drive into town. Winnie smiled to herself as she remembered Howard learning to drive and how he had run into the gas pump at Mr. Hall's store. Her other brothers, Brandon, Kyle and Nathan, hadn't let him forget that!

Howard carefully maneuvered the car through the streets of town. Finally they came to a stop in front of a big old house. It was not like any house Winnie had ever seen. It was big, but then so was the house Winnie lived in. But this house was different. "Oh, yes," Winnie thought, "it's an elegant house."

Winnie had read about elegant houses but she had never seen one. It stood tall and straight, with windows that bowed out in front and towers that seemed to reach to the sky. There were stately brick chimneys with smoke curling from them. All around the edge of the roof was lacy white trim. It looked like the gingerbread house Aunt Lucy had brought for Christmas. "Is this what an apartment looks like?" Winnie pondered.

"Now, Winnie, make sure you take off your boots at the door," Howard warned as they made their way along the path cut with precision through the snow banks. "And, Winnie," Howard continued, "don't blurt out anything we'll all regret later!"

Winnie knew she'd have no trouble with her boots but whether or not she could keep her tongue still she wasn't quite certain.

Howard pushed a little button beside the door and a musical tune played from somewhere within. Winnie's eyes were wide and her heart beat rapidly. The door opened and Aunt Ann greeted them warmly.

"She looks elegant too," Winnie thought, "just like the house." Her soft brown hair was pulled back sleekly from her face. Lovely tortoise-shell combs held loose strands in place. A lacy collar was fastened with a gold and amber broach under Aunt Ann's chin.

Winnie removed her boots and she and Howard followed Aunt Ann into what appeared to Winnie as something out of a dream. A coal fire glowed softly in a brick fireplace. A copper kettle, freshly polished, shone on the hearth, boiling the water for tea. A quaint little couch like one Winnie had seen in a book about the King and Queen sat facing the fireplace. A desk, tables and pretty little chairs dotted the room, giving the appearance of a world far removed from Winnie's.

Winnie and Howard were ushered to the beautiful couch with its rich fabric and carved wood. Aunt Ann called it a "settee." Winnie tried to sit as straight and tall as she could. Howard, she noticed, was doing the same. Even so, he looked a little awkward. Aunt Ann took the shiny kettle from the hearth and went to make tea.

Winnie looked up. Grandma was standing in the doorway with her arms open wide and a quiet smile on her face. Howard and Winnie tripped over one another in an effort to reach Grandma first.

Winnie stepped back, looking hard at Grandma. She was wearing the blue housedress with little white flowers that Mamma had made for her birthday. Over top was the pink apron Hope had given Grandma for Christmas. Her pretty white hair was tied back as usual. Everything about Grandma looked the same as Winnie remembered. But something was wrong!

Aunt Ann came in with a tray. She set it on the table. Winnie admired the little china teapot with matching cups and saucers, a pretty flowered plate with store-bought cookies and the crystal glass of milk for her. Winnie carefully took the milk and cookies. It all seemed so lovely but something was not right. Winnie could feel it in her heart.

Winnie mused as Howard struggled to get his big fingers around the tiny cup handle. She'd have lots of things to tell Mary Beth when she got home. "This evening should be so perfect," Winnie told herself. But deep within was a gnawing uneasiness and it wouldn't go away.

Suddenly, Winnie jumped to her feet. "I know what's wrong," she blurted forth. Howard glanced sternly toward her. But there was no stopping Winnie. "Grandma," she said, "you don't belong here. You don't fit in. Everything here is so elegant just like Aunt Ann, but you belong at home with us!"

"Oh, dear, what have I done?" bemoaned Winnie to herself. "Howard told me to keep my tongue out of trouble. Oh, what have I done?" Winnie dared look at Grandma. Grandma was looking softly at her. Tears welled in Grandma's beautiful blue eyes and Winnie saw one roll down her cheek. Winnie hadn't meant to make Grandma sad. It had all slipped out so quickly.

Aunt Ann stood up, walked to the other end of the room and back again. "Winnie's right, Flossie, dear. It was selfish of me to take you from your home and family and expect you to fit into my life. You must go home with Howard and Winnie tonight. I won't be lonely if you promise to visit."

Winnie could hardly believe her ears. The ache was gone from her heart. She looked at Grandma and the sparkle was back in her eyes. Aunt Ann went off with Grandma to help pack her things. Winnie looked at Howard with apprehension wondering if she was really in trouble.

"Well," Howard chuckled, "for once, Winnie, your tongue wagged at the right time. Grandma's coming home."

"Winnie and the Big Kids"
Vankoughnet, Muskoka, circa 1950's

"A QUIET REPOSE"

Winnie was exasperated. "I am never coming out of here!" she stated emphatically.

"Now, Winnie," she could hear Mamma in her most encouraging voice, "you come out of there right now."

"I'm never coming out!" Winnie responded with defiance in her voice.

"What do you expect to eat in there, Winnie?" She could hear Howard, her oldest brother, chiming into the conversation.

She knew most of the family, except for her dad and uncles, of course, were standing outside the door. Winnie had locked herself inside the bathroom and she wasn't coming out.

"At least tell me what is upsetting you, Winnie," Mamma pleaded.

Winnie rarely, if ever, disobeyed Mamma. She felt a little guilty in doing so now. But Winnie was so angry with her older brothers Brandon, Kyle and Nathan. They teased her about everything.

"You're going to marry Trent Mingey someday!" Winnie was horrified.

"Don't you dare say that to me," she responded.
"Winnie have you ever heard yourself sing?" another one chimed in.

"Winnie, you could trip over your own shadow."

"It's your turn to do the dishes, Winnie."

"Can't you even catch a ball, Winnie?"

On and on it went. Winnie had had enough! Sometimes when things overwhelmed Winnie, she would shut herself in the bathroom for a little while until she calmed down. But this was different. This time she was never coming out!

Winnie lived in the little village of Mistymeadow with her mother and father, her five brothers, two sisters, two uncles and her grandmother. There weren't many quiet moments in Winnie's life. And then Aunt Ann, Grandma's twin sister, had come to stay at Winnie's house for a while. Why there was hardly enough room in their house now without adding another person.

"Where on earth will we put her?" Winnie had asked her mother, thinking that the back porch might be a good place.

"Well, dear," Mamma had said, "you and Mary Beth will have to move into Hope's room. She is only home on weekends and Aunt Ann can have your room."

Winnie didn't want to believe what Mamma was saying.

"Give up our room?" Winnie wailed in total disbelief. "But Mary Beth and I love our room," she continued.

"I know, dear, but Aunt Ann needs a place to stay for a few months until she can find a home of her own in town."

"A few months," Winnie grumbled. "It will probably be forever!"

Winnie felt she had lost her focus. She and Mary Beth shared a room. It wasn't a big room but it was theirs. It had two windows, one that faced the creek and one that looked out over the village of Mistymeadow.

Aunt Eileen, Mamma's sister, had sent a big box of used clothing to Winnie's house. "Too small for my girls," she had said. "Try them on Winnie and Mary Beth." Amidst the articles of clothing was a wonderful big piece of material. Mamma had made curtains with ruffles for the windows and a cover to match for their bed. It was a rosy colour with white and blue and yellow flowers with green leaves on it.

Winnie and Mary Beth shared a dresser: the top two drawers were for Winnie and the bottom two were for Mary Beth. The middle drawer had a divider inside it. On one side were Winnie's treasures and on the other were Mary Beth's. There was an old armchair in the corner and Grandma had knit a pretty blue afghan to cover it. The walls of the room were "a delicate blue," Mamma said. Mary Beth and Winnie had their books and few toys scattered about. Winnie's favourite reading spot was in the old armchair with her teddy bear perched beside her. She could curl up with a book and not even know what the rest of the world was doing.

Then Aunt Ann had arrived with her trunk, leather luggage with straps, and millinery boxes piled sky-high. Winnie's room was gone. She and Mary Beth had collected their clothes and a few toys and books and moved into Hope's room.

"Nothing ever stays the same," bemoaned Winnie.

"Enough of this nonsense, Winnie! You come out of that bathroom this minute!" Winnie could hear the impatience in Mamma's voice.

"Just leave her there. She'll get over it, whatever it is," Winnie could hear her brother's voice again. "She'll come out when she's hungry."

"They can send my food up the laundry chute," Winnie thought to herself. "I'll starve before I come out of here!"

Everything went silent outside the bathroom door. Winnie put her ear up to the door, but she couldn't hear a thing. "Where was everyone? Didn't they realize she was still in here? Didn't anyone know that she hadn't had anything to eat since breakfast?"

Winnie opened the little door of the laundry chute. The chute led from the bathroom down into a cupboard in the back kitchen. Winnie listened carefully. The voices were muffled but she could hear sounds coming from the kitchen. She listened some more and suddenly she could smell some good aromas.

"They're having lunch!" Winnie thought indignantly. "Here I am in here with all my problems and they are having lunch! Nobody understands and nobody cares!" Winnie felt abandoned.

A gentle knock sounded on the bathroom door. Winnie could hear Grandma's quiet voice. "Winnie dear, may I come in?" Winnie knew that Grandma was always there for her and she could not say no to Grandma's request. "It's just me," Grandma continued. "The others are having their lunch."

Winnie turned the key in the lock and slowly opened the door. Grandma looked directly at Winnie with her soft blue eyes. "Closing yourself off from the world doesn't make your problems go away," Grandma said quietly. "Maybe if I come in we can talk a little bit about what's bothering you, Winnie." Grandma eased her way in the door and sat on the edge of the bathtub.

"Your brothers have teased you many times before and you have never been this upset about it. Talk to me, Winnie."

Winnie didn't really know where to begin. "It's not just the teasing," Winnie admitted. "It's that I don't have a place just for me."

"What do you mean, Winnie?" Grandma urged her.

"I don't have anywhere to go to get away from everyone. There is no place to go to be quiet." Winnie felt shy telling Grandma this.

"I used to have my room with my books and chair and only Mary Beth to share it. But now Aunt Ann has my room and she calls it her room. Yesterday she told Mary Beth she could come into her room and use the little desk she had Daddy put in there for her."

"Go on, Winnie," Grandma encouraged.

"Well, this morning I thought I would use Aunt Ann's little desk. Aunt Ann came in when I was sitting there. 'What are you doing in here, Winnie?' she asked. 'I gave Mary Beth permission to come in here but I don't recall saying anything to you!'"

Winnie began sobbing as she related the incident to Grandma. Grandma was very quiet and her head was bowed. Then she lifted her head and looked straight at Winnie.

"I understand completely what you are saying, Winnie. I like to have some quiet time in my day too. But I also need to tell you about Aunt Ann. She has lived on her own for many years. She never married and had children. So we may need to be a little patient with her until we all get used to one another.

Winnie took a deep breath.

"As far as your brothers are concerned," Grandma continued, "I'll speak to your mother and father and I am sure they'll have them ease up on the teasing."

Winnie felt her confidence returning. She wiped her eyes, washed her face, and together she and Grandma emerged to face the world.

Later that day Winnie's brothers came to her, one by one.

"Sorry for teasing you, Winnie."

"Sorry, Winnie."
"Won't do it again, Winnie!"

Winnie knew that they would tease her again but it felt good to have them say they were sorry.

That evening Winnie and Mary Beth were about to jump into bed when Aunt Ann appeared at the door. "Hello, you two," she called out in a cheerful voice. "I have something for each of you."

Winnie and Mary Beth scrambled to see what it was. Aunt Ann gave Mary Beth a pretty little box with tiny elephants on it. And for Winnie she had a beautiful gold pin with an amber stone.

"It's something you can wear when you are all grown-up," she said to Winnie. "I wanted to thank you both for allowing me to use your room for a little while." Winnie and Mary Beth gave Aunt Ann a big hug and they all said goodnight.

The next morning life went on as usual. Mary Beth and Winnie had chores to do and the older boys went off to help Winnie's dad pile some wood. Winnie's little brother, Evan, was working with Aunt Ann putting together a little puzzle she had brought for him.

"Winnie," Grandma called from upstairs. "Can you come here for a minute, please?" Winnie dropped her dust cloth and ran to see what Grandma wanted.

"Come into my room, Winnie." Grandma reached for Winnie's hand and drew her into the bedroom. There underneath the window Grandma had placed a little pine table and covered it with a pretty cloth she had embroidered herself. On top of the table was a glass lamp with flowers painted on it and pushed up to the table was a small chair with a pink cushion. Winnie looked at Grandma with expectant eyes.

"Sometimes," Grandma said, "we all need a place for quiet repose. I've found this little spot in my room and I want to share it with you. Whenever you need to get away from everything for a little while, you may come in here."

Winnie felt the weight of the last few days lift completely. "Thank you, Grandma," she said as she moved into the room to try out the little table and chair.

"A Golden Glow"
Vankoughnet, Muskoka, circa 1950's

"A GOLDEN GLOW"

Drip, drip, drip! Winnie watched mesmerized as the snow slowly melted from the roof above her bedroom window. The warmth of the sun bathed her face through the glass pane. She could hear her father rummaging in the eaves of the attic of their house. He was gathering the sap cans together and looking for the straining cloths and all the other things he had stored in there since last spring.

Winnie felt a ripple of excitement. Today was the day that her father and Uncle Cecil and Uncle Will, along with her older brothers when their schooling would permit, would tap the trees to make maple syrup. Winnie had thought the winter would never end. Morning after morning she and Mary Beth would get dressed under the covers because it was too chilly to step out of bed with just their night-clothes on.

One morning when she and Mary Beth were walking to school, Mary Beth got tears in her eyes from the bitter cold. Her eyelids froze completely shut. Little Mary Beth had cried even harder and made the situation worse.

"What should she do?" Winnie worried. Her older brothers had left earlier. They had to get to school to bring in the day's wood and build the warm fire in the wood stove.

Winnie remembered Aunt Mae, who lived about half way between Winnie's house and the school, had said one time, "Children, if you ever need a refuge on your way to school, remember I am almost always at home."

Winnie could see Aunt Mae's house down the road. She knew she would have to guide Mary Beth there. Aunt Mae had welcomed them warmly, both with her kindness and also the warmth of the wood stove. She brought a soft towel and gently wiped Mary Beth's eyes. When the girls were sufficiently warmed Aunt Mae gave them each a hug and sent them on their way. Aunt Mae was married to Grandma's brother, Uncle Ned, but Winnie thought she was a lot like Grandma. It was her gentleness, she supposed.

Winnie shook herself. What was the matter with her? One minute she was busy doing something and suddenly she was drawn somewhere different in her mind. "That child spends more time daydreaming than she does anything else," Uncle Will often said.

Winnie dashed downstairs. Already Mamma was pulling three large loaves of home-made bread from the oven. Three more looking like over stuffed turkeys were waiting to go in. Everything smelled so good: the aroma of the fresh bread, the smell of the wood fire in the cook stove, and the pot of fresh coffee Mamma was perking on the stove.

It was a day to feel good. Winnie had brought home three library books to read. The snow was melting, so spring was very near. Her dad had begun to make maple syrup and Winnie loved that. Suddenly the world was taking on a golden glow.

Just then Trent Mingey, the boy who lived across the road from Winnie, appeared at the door. Usually he walked right in and made himself at home. Winnie figured he must think that there were so many kids here already, what was one more? But today Trent Mingey wasn't himself. Winnie noticed it immediately.

"What's wrong with you?" she queried.
"None of your business," Trent retorted.

Trent may not think it any of her business but Winnie intended to make it so. She wasn't used to Trent being so sullen.

"Want to play "Snakes and Ladders" with me?" She knew that was his favourite game, so maybe he'd get so interested in it he'd forget himself and tell Winnie what was bothering him. They rolled the die and counted out the spaces, up the ladders and down the snakes. Trent didn't budge, not one word as to what was on his mind.

After lunch Mamma sent them off to the sap bush with hot coffee and a loaf of bread for Daddy and the others. "You two need some fresh air," she said. "You've been hanging around this house all morning."

Winnie's dad and uncles already had the spiles tapped into the trees and the sap was beginning to drip into the pails. Uncle Will was in the sap house stoking a big fire in the separator. "We don't need this going just yet," he said, "but I want to make sure everything is up and running for the big boil."

Trent hardly said a word.

"What's bothering Trent?" Winnie's dad questioned her when they were a little distance away.

"He won't tell me," Winnie replied.

"Well, we must respect that," Winnie's dad said. "He'll tell us when he is good and ready."

Being patient wasn't one of Winnie's stronger qualities. She felt Trent would be ready to talk sooner rather than later.

The sun was beginning to disappear over the tree line and there was a chill in the air. "Winnie, you and Trent better get yourselves on home now," her father called out. "And with all the mild weather this afternoon the ice may be ready to crack on the creek, so don't go near it!" he cautioned.

Winnie shivered as she trudged along beside Trent. He was still uncommonly quiet. Winnie didn't know how to reach him.

"Better leave it for another day," she conceded to herself.

"I'm going home this way," Trent mumbled under his breath and started across the creek on a shortcut home.

"No, Trent," Winnie tried to grab his jacket. "Daddy said it's not safe."

"Yeah, well he's always warning us about something, and he's not my dad anyway, so I don't have to do what he says."

Trent was definitely in a mood and not to be reckoned with.
"You'll be sorry."

No sooner were the words out of her mouth than Trent Mingey broke through the ice. Winnie looked on in horror. Trent flailed and sputtered and gasped. Winnie knew the water wasn't deep and if Trent just put his feet down he would be standing on the bottom of the creek.

"Just stand up!" Winnie called out.

But Trent wasn't listening. He was in a state of near panic. Winnie could run for help or she could shout as loud as she could, but she was too far away from the house and no one was around to hear.

Winnie grabbed a big alder branch that had broken off in some previous windstorm. "Here, Trent, hold on to this," she called out in the calmest voice she could muster. Trent obediently reached for the alder branch and with Winnie pulling on one end and him holding on to the other she guided him to shore.

Trent was shivering and shaking from head to toe when they entered the back kitchen of Winnie's house. "Goodness gracious, child!" Mamma exclaimed when she saw the wet clothes and the shivering little body. "Whatever happened to you?"

Mamma quickly whisked Trent over by the wood fire. "Winnie, run and get some of Nathan's clothes."

Grandma came with a big, warm afghan and bound Trent right up in it. "Now you just stay there young man while I go and call your mother," Grandma said in a firm voice.

"She won't care what's happened to me," Trent retorted.

"Whatever do you mean, child?" Grandma asked in her kindest voice. In the meantime Mamma was on the phone to Mrs. Mingey.

Trent began to sob and with his voice coming out in short, little spurts he revealed what was bothering him. "My mother and father are going to take in kids who aren't really part of our family," Trent blurted out. "And they probably won't love me anymore," he continued.

"Oh, Trent, child," Grandma put her arm around him and consoled him. "Look at all the children in this household. There is love enough for all and lots to spare. Your family will always love you."
Winnie stood quietly in the background, but she couldn't help hearing the conversation.

"Trent," Grandma continued softly, "love comes from God and when we know God loves us we have lots of love to share with others too. You're mother and father know how much God loves them and they have enough love for you and your brothers and lots left over to share with any other children who might come into your home."

Trent's sobs were subsiding. Just then the door burst open.

"Good heavens, child, are you all right?" Mrs. Mingey broke the quietness of the moment. She ran to Trent and threw her arms around him. "I was worried sick when Winnie's mother called."

"I'm okay, now," Trent said sheepishly as he leaned his head on his mother's shoulder. "I had so many things on my mind and I wasn't being careful like Winnie's dad told me to be. I tried to cross the creek and the ice wasn't safe."

"What on earth do you have on your mind?" Trent's mother continued.

Trent poured out his whole story of how he thought his mother and father wouldn't love him as much once they had the foster children to look after.

"Oh, Trent," she said kindly, "you are my child. No one could ever take your place! I love you, Trent, and I always will."

Winnie noticed the tears in Mrs. Mingey's eyes.

"I love you too, Mamma," Trent replied.

Winnie's mother helped Mrs. Mingey bundle Trent up against the cold air and sent them off home. Winnie went upstairs to get her cozy night-clothes on before having her supper. She looked out her window. The little drips from early in the day had frozen into tiny icicles and there was just a hint of pink left in the evening sky.

Grandma appeared at her doorway. "Are you all right, Winnie dear?"

"I'm okay, Grandma," she replied.

"I'm proud of you, Winnie. You did well today. You took control and gave Trent the assistance he needed. Sometimes we tell you that you daydream too much, Winnie, but when the situation demands it you come through with flying colours."

Winnie smiled at Grandma. She sensed that golden glow once again but this time it was in her heart.

That night around the supper table the conversation turned to the events of the day. Winnie sat quietly and listened.

"Could have been a different story if Winnie hadn't been there."

"Wouldn't take long to freeze your limbs in that cold air."

"Good thing Trent's going to be okay."

Winnie didn't say anything. She just knew it had been a good day.

Mamma's Homemade Bread

3 pkgs. of fast rising dry yeast - Prepare yeast according to directions on pkg. In a large bread pan put 1 cup shortening, a little less than a 1/2 cup sugar and about a 1/4 cup salt.

8 cups of water - Pour 4 cups of boiling water over the shortening, sugar and salt and stir until shortening is melted. Add remaining 4 cups of cold water making the whole amount lukewarm.

Then add the yeast which has risen and been stirred. Now begin to add flour gradually, beating with a large wooden spoon. Continue to add flour and beat until the mixture is too stiff to beat.

Now add more flour gradually and begin kneading with your hands. Add flour and knead until the dough is not sticky. Form into a ball. Keep kneading, pulling the dough from the sides of the pan and working it into the centre. Grease the sides of the pan and the top of the dough. Put the lid on the pan and cover with a cloth. The pan must be kept from draughts.

Let rise at room temperature until well doubled in bulk. Punch it down and let it rise again. Then form into loaves. This amount should make 7 large loaves. Put loaves in greased pans and grease tops with a little butter. Cover and let rise until well doubled.

Bake at 375 degrees. When done turn out on rack or upside down on bake board. Rub tops with a little soft butter. Do not store until bread is cold.

"The Lumber Mill"
Vankoughnet, Muskoka, circa 1950's

"CHANGING TIMES - AN EPILOGUE"

Winnie felt strange. Things were happening to her over which she had no control. Her legs seemed longer and ganglier than ever. Some parts of her body were changing in strange and unusual ways. And just yesterday she noticed a little blemish on her chin,

"Oh, that's just a pimple," Kyle, her older brother, had announced to the whole family much to Winnie's chagrin. Winnie knew it wasn't a pimple because never in her whole life did she intend to have such a thing.

"Mamma, can you measure me?" she said as she stood with her back against the doorframe and held her head high.

The inside of the doorframe in the kitchen of the house in Mistymeadow where Winnie lived with all her family was covered with marks. The height that she, and her brothers and sisters, had achieved at varying times in their lives was depicted by these marks.

"My, you are on a growing spree," Mamma exclaimed as she penciled a mark at Winnie's new height. "Why you've grown four whole inches since we measured you the last time."

Winnie didn't mind getting taller but it was these other unusual symptoms that were bothering her.

Winnie was excited. Christos, the young man who had been the student minister at their little village church during the summers, had asked Winnie's older sister, Hope, if she would be his bride. After a lot of quiet conversation to which Winnie was not privy, Hope and Christos became engaged. Hope asked Winnie to be a junior bridesmaid. She wasn't quite sure what a junior bridesmaid did, but she was thrilled to think Hope had confidence that Winnie could handle it.

Aunt Ann, Grandma's twin sister, had passed away earlier in the year. Winnie sometimes saw a sadness in Grandma's eyes. Lately Winnie would remember Aunt Ann saying that Winnie was "growing toward adolescence." Winnie didn't like that word very much but she had a funny little feeling that Aunt Ann's prediction was coming true.

The summer was turning out to be a very hot one. "A real scorcher," Uncle Cecil put it.

Winnie and Mary Beth had lots of chores to do. "You girls can sweep the floors and do the dusting and make certain the table is set for supper," Mamma informed them. And, of course, it went without saying that the dishes were to be done after meals. Mary Beth and Winnie constantly argued over who would wash and who would dry.

Winnie's house was a flurry of activity. Hope was home every weekend. Invitations had to be sent, food to be decided on, and dresses to be made. On and on it went. Hope hardly had time to spend with Winnie anymore.

"Any free time she has, she needs to be spending it with her future husband," Mamma explained.

"Here we go again," bemoaned Winnie, "another big change." But since Winnie really liked Christos she thought this change wouldn't be so bad.

"Winnie, I need you to try on your dress before I go any further."

Mamma was making Winnie's dress for Hope's wedding. Winnie's older cousins Joyce and Lise were the maid of honour and bridesmaid. Their dresses, along with Winnie's, were made out of beautiful material called peau de soie. Winnie thought she couldn't be anything but elegant in a dress made of that material.

The lumber mill was running at full tilt. Daddy and Winnie's uncles and older brothers were working long hours every day. All the row upon row of logs they had taken out of the bush in winter had to be sawn into lumber and shipped off to various parts of the country. Kyle and Nathan, along with Uncle Cecil, used the cant hooks to roll the logs into the mill; Uncle Will was in the edger pen; Brandon and Howard helped Daddy on the trimmer, while their cousin Rob was the experienced sawyer.

Rob had worked for Winnie's dad since he was a young boy. "Most dependable man I've got," Daddy would say. The entire mill was run by an old steam engine that was well oiled and fine tuned by longtime engineer Harry Rhysler.

The men would come home after a long day and the boys would head straight for the Misty River to swim away the day's dust and exhaustion. Winnie's dad and Uncle Cecil and Uncle Will would sit one by one on a chair at the back door and remove their boots, turn down their cuffs, and shake their pants. Each one left a little stash of sawdust. Uncle Cecil would get the broom and dustpan and sweep up every speck.

"Winnie, are you coming?" Mamma called out in a little louder voice.

Winnie thumped down the stairs. She used to have a lighter step, she thought to herself.

"Do I have to try it on?" Winnie asked, feeling it was so hot she would never get the dress off again.
"I think you had better, just to make certain this strapless design is suitable for you."

Winnie was feeling very grown-up indeed, wearing the very same style gown as the older attendants. She went into the bathroom and came out with the dress on. But the expression on her face was anything but ecstatic. She had her thumbs and fingers holding up each side of her dress just in front of her armpits.

"Mamma," she exclaimed, "this dress won't stay up on me."

At that precise moment Kyle, Winnie's brother most likely to tease, walked through the door. One glance at Winnie and a huge grin spread over his face. "Hey, that's an easy problem to solve, Winnie. Just wear the dress backwards and your shoulder blades will hold it up."

With that he ran off to share the incident with his brothers. Winnie was devastated. Her hope of wearing the same style as the older girls was shattered. She ran to the bathroom, tore the dress off, and handed it back to Mamma. Winnie went up to her room and closed the door.

The dinner hour came and went and neither Mamma nor Grandma attempted to get Winnie to come downstairs. As the evening progressed the older boys went off to play ball. Winnie emerged from her room and came downstairs. Her eyes were swollen from crying but neither Mamma nor Grandma mentioned that either.

The heat wave continued. The little creek that Winnie loved so much was almost dried to nothing. Water had to be carried from the well for the animals. Even the Misty River, about which Winnie's dad continually warned that a deep current always ran through it, was so low you could see the sandy bottom.

Winnie felt so hot sometimes the perspiration ran down her body. She hoped that was the heat wave and not another one of these changes she had been noticing. Trent Mingey didn't come over nearly as often. Since Winnie had taken this great growing spurt, she was now several inches taller than he and he didn't seem nearly as interested in playing with her.

One afternoon the air was so still the dragonflies sat dormant on the rail fence. The birds were silent and the only sound in the air was the monotonous humming of the summer bugs. Winnie and Mary Beth were playing together under the silver maple in the front corner of the yard. They had taken a little table and chairs outside and were having lemonade. Evan was playing quietly in his sandbox, while Mamma and Grandma sat on the veranda shelling peas. The stillness and the heat gave an ominous feel to the day. The whole world seemed to Winnie to be in slow motion.

They could hear it long before they could see it. Suddenly, an old blue pickup truck rattled at an enormous speed along the road and turned into the lane. Winnie and Mary Beth, startled by the noise, ran to Mamma. Little Evan began to cry. Grandma quickly went and swooped him up.

Luke Dannah, Daddy's longtime hired hand, jumped from the truck. "Where are the men?" he shouted. "The old place is on fire!"

Grandma and Mamma stood shocked. "They're all at the mill except for Howard and Brandon. They are in the barn doing some repairs."

Without another word he jumped back into the truck, then called out the window to Mamma, "Start the phonin.' We'll need everyone we can get. I'm headin' back down!"

"Winnie," Mamma's voice was high pitched, "run like the wind and get Howard and Brandon! They'll stop at the mill and get the others on the way to the fire."

Winnie ran like she'd never run before. Brandon was on the roof of the chicken coop and Howard was in the barn. "Howard! Brandon! Come quick! The old place is on fire! Mamma said you have to tell Daddy and the others on your way!"

The look on Winnie's face expressed immediately to her brothers the seriousness of the situation. They took off for home at a full gallop. The only vehicle in the yard was the family car. They looked at Mamma for permission to take it.

"Just go!" she said. "On a day like today that fire will be out of control in no time. Winnie, you run to the Mingey's and the Hall's and tell anyone you can find to help out. Grandma's already on the phone."

Winnie ran so hard she could hardly breath. Everyone she spoke to responded immediately. Cars and trucks and tractors, well any vehicles that would move, were heading down the road toward the old place. The "old place" was the farm where Winnie's family had lived before her dad had built this new house. It was on the outskirts of the village, but with the dryness in the earth it wouldn't take long for the fire to reach the homes in the village. Mistymeadow had not had a big fire in all the years since Winnie could remember. But she had heard her dad and uncles talk about the devastation of one many years before.

The lull of the afternoon changed to a pitch of immediate urgency. Mrs. Mingey came running in the door followed shortly by Mrs. Hall and several other neighbour ladies. "We've brought bread and meat and eggs. We'll make up some sandwiches and cold drinks and coffee for the men."

Mamma's kitchen was abuzz with activity. Winnie and Mary Beth were in charge of making the cold drinks. Lemonade was their speciality so they made it by the gallon. Mamma always kept lots of lemons and lots of sugar on hand in the summertime.

The smell of smoke wafted through the still air. Trent Mingey, wanting so much to be helpful, suggested he ride his bicycle just close enough to see what was happening.

"Well, you stay away from the fire," his mother cautioned sharply, "and tell the men that we have food here for them when someone can come and get it."

Trent was gone like a shot. Having an important task to do gave him an air of superiority. He glanced back at Winnie but Winnie did not respond. Somehow Trent Mingey didn't irritate her quite as much as he used to. One of the men came and retrieved the food and drinks.

"How are things going?" Grandma asked him quietly.

"Not out yet," he grunted.

Trent Mingey returned safely with great stories of how high the blaze was and the distance it was covering. "There are men everywhere. They've come from all over Oak Leaf Township, a lot from Gruffington, and even some from Silver Bridge. They're digging big ditches all around the fire," he reported.

"That will contain it in one area," Grandma explained. "They hope it will burn itself out and not reach the village."

One by one as the evening progressed, the ladies went off to their respective homes. Mamma and Grandma made more sandwiches knowing their men would be hungry when they got home. Winnie and Mary Beth wanted to stay up all night. Little Evan had already fallen asleep on the sofa and Mamma had carried him off to bed.

"You two go on up now and snuggle in," Mamma said.

"But, Mamma, we don't want to miss anything," Winnie protested.

"Don't worry, child, if there is any change we will let you know."

Winnie had a hard time to get to sleep. Mary Beth's head hardly hit the pillow and she was out. Winnie tossed and turned and eventually fell asleep.

It was still dark out when Winnie heard Mamma's voice. "Wake up, children, your father wants to show us something."

Winnie shook Mary Beth and they both scrambled to get dressed and go downstairs. Daddy was in the kitchen eating a sandwich and drinking coffee. He was covered in soot from head to toe.

"The fire is basically out; the threat is gone anyway. But there's a sight I want you to see," he reported.

Everyone bundled into the family car and drove to the "old place". Winnie had never seen such an amazing scene. The fire was out but every stump on the large area of burned land was still ablaze. The appearance was that of a huge Indian village with many bonfires burning brightly. Winnie looked at Grandma and there were tears in her eyes. Winnie snuggled her hand into Grandma's.

"The land is burned over but the heart of the land is still alive," Grandma said quietly to herself. Winnie wasn't really sure what she meant but she thought she was referring to the fact that the land would come to life again.

The stories of the fire were told over and over many times in the little village of Mistymeadow and far beyond. The bravery of the men, the quick response on the part of so many people, and the kindness shown to Winnie's family would not soon be forgotten.

Life slowly returned to a normal pace. The heat wave ended and wonderful cool breezes swept through the village. Hope's wedding was fast approaching. Winnie's dress was finished and hung with a big, white sheet over it in Grandma's closet. Mamma had solved the problem of the strapless gown by adding pretty little "shoe-string" straps, she called them, over the shoulders. Winnie was happy.

Hope's wedding day dawned clear and bright. Hope had curled Winnie's hair and, although it was a little frizzy, Winnie could live with it. Mamma had bought Winnie her very first pair of nylon stockings and shoes with a small heel on them. Little by little Winnie was accepting the changes.

Hope was beautiful in her white wedding gown and Christos was the handsome groom with his dark hair and strong features. The wedding was in Silver Bridge where Mamma and Daddy were married many years before. The day was "picture perfect," Winnie thought as she observed the entire scene.

Winnie stood straight and tall, her peau de soie gown blowing gently in the breeze, her high heels and nylon stockings actually feeling comfortable. She took a deep breath. "Maybe adolescence isn't so bad after all."

Just then Winnie's brother Kyle came strolling by. He glanced at Winnie and then stopped to take a second look. "You look amazing, Winnie! I can hardly believe it's you."

Winnie smiled. "I think that was a compliment," she said to herself.

Winnie walked over and stood beside Grandma. "Someday this will be you, Winnie," Grandma said. "You'll find that special someone and share your life with him."

Winnie couldn't even imagine it. "Right now, Grandma, I'm having a hard enough time just thinking about growing up." Winnie thought she heard Grandma actually giggle.

"Just remember, Winnie, live from your heart and these other things will take care of themselves," Grandma reminded her.